BURN THE DEAD

QUARANTINE

STEVEN JENKINS

First published in The USA in 2014
by Black Bed Sheet Books
Published in Great Britain in 2015
by Different Cloud Publishing.
www.steven-jenkins.com

CONTENTS

Burn the dead : quarantine.
\<cjg\>

"For Vicky."

FREE BOOK

"If you love scary campfire stories of ghosts, demonology, and all things that go bump in the night, then you'll love this horror collection by author Steven Jenkins."

COLIN DAVIES – Director of BAFTA winning BBC's The Coalhouse.

For a limited time only, you can download a **FREE** copy of Spine - the latest horror collection from Steven Jenkins.

FIND OUT MORE HERE

1

Another day. Another dollar.

However fulfilling a job might be, nothing feels quite like finishing after a twelve-hour day.

I punch the six-digit code into the panel, and the steel door closes behind me, letting out a shrill, squeaking noise as it locks into place.

The late shifts are a killer—especially in the winter. There's something very depressing and just plain *wrong* about starting and finishing work in complete darkness. Still, the extra cash is a plus. Money's tight all 'round. Vegas is just three short weeks away, and I still haven't saved a thing. Not a single penny. And worse still, Tommy is on my back to settle up the flight costs.

Good luck with that Tommy-boy!

At the staff car park, I feel the cold air on my cheeks as I pull out my keys from my jacket pocket, buried deep among the loose change, petrol receipts, and expired lottery tickets. I climb into the car and check my phone; still no signal. Shaking my head in annoyance, I pull away, flashing my ID badge to

Smithy at the gates, and then I'm off.

About a quarter of a mile from Romkirk, I hear my phone make a beeping sound in my pocket. *Finally*, a signal. I mean really, how can there still be places where you can't get phone reception? For God's sake, they can speak to a man on the bloody moon—surely Bristol shouldn't be a problem. I contemplate reading the text, but know who it is: it's Anna, wondering where the hell I am. Don't want to waste any more time pulling over to read it. I just want to get home.

To bed.

* * *

I manage to make the thirty-five-mile drive to Crandale in less than fifty minutes, thanks to it being so late—but mainly thanks to breaking the speed limit for ninety percent of the journey. Lucky for me, I know exactly where all the cameras are— hidden or not.

Pulling up outside my house, I notice the blinds are closed in Sammy's bedroom. *Missed another bedtime*. This'll be the third this week, not counting the other six from last week. I sigh loudly as I climb out of the car and walk up to the house. I see Edith May from next door again, staring out of her living-room window. I give her my usual wave, and she returns the gesture. *Nosy old cow*. I bet she's judging me, all these late finishes. I bet she thinks I'm a terrible father.

Is she right?

"You're home late, Rob," Anna points out as I enter the kitchen. "How was work?"

I fling my jacket over the back of the dining chair, and then walk up to her. "It was fine. Usual stuff. Just a bit tired."

I wrap my arms around Anna's thin waist and pull her close to kiss her. She then pulls away, making a face. "I think you need a shower, Hun," she tells me. "You *stink*."

I lift an arm up over my head and sniff my armpit. She's right. Twelve hours stuck in that tiny little room with no air-conditioning will do that to you. "Yeah I know. Long day. You'd stink too."

"Yeah, yeah, we know."

"Did you find the bloody dog yet?"

Anna shakes her head. "No. I've looked everywhere. Me and Sammy walked the whole of Crandale. Can't find her anywhere."

"Shit. That *bloody dog*. I knew it was a mistake getting one for him. I *knew it*. What did I say from day one?" I run my fingers through my short brown hair and groan. *Stupid dog*. "How's Sammy taking it?"

"How'd ya think? He's devastated. I had to lie to him. I said she's just playing hide and seek. I told him that she'll get bored soon and come home."

"Oh well, he's only four. I'm sure he'll forget. If not, we'll have to buy him a new one. Preferably one *without* any legs." I raise my arms up, yawning loudly. "I'll help you look for her tomorrow. Not tonight though. I'm so tired my eyes are burning."

"Yeah, that's fine. I'm sure she'll turn up somewhere. Have you eaten yet?

I let out a fake chuckle. "What do *you* think?"

"So that's a no then I take it?"

"*Yep*. Well, unless you count the bar of chocolate I had at four-thirty."

Anna shakes her head. "That's not right. You

10

should complain to your supervisor. They should hire someone to cover you. Or at least some admin staff. Take some of the paperwork off your shoulders. Doesn't the law say that employers have to give you a break every four hours or something?"

"Probably. But you know what that place is like. Everything's got to be done *yesterday*. And as for speaking to my boss, I've already tried. We *all* have. It's just in one ear, and out the other with him. There's nothing much I can do at the moment. I've just got to suck it up. But the worst thing about it is not taking Sammy to bed. *Again*. I mean, I can handle missing the odd meal and writing up *endless* reports. And I can even handle having a shitty boss. But not spending time with Sammy—it bloody kills me. It really does."

"Yeah, I know. Must be horrible. Well, maybe you need to find another job then. Something with more sociable hours. Like a postman."

I let out a small laugh and then shake my head. "No, it's fine. I'm sure I'll survive. It won't be like this forever. And it *is* a great job. It's just hard sometimes. Like most jobs."

"Well, it's not right." Anna opens the fridge and pulls out a large container, and then places it on the kitchen worktop. "Still got some pasta left over. But I wouldn't have this if I were you."

"Why?" I ask, peering down at the chicken, pasta and pesto. "Looks good. What's wrong with it?"

"Well, I had some earlier and now my stomach doesn't feel right. I think I may have undercooked the chicken. Better not risk it. I'll make you something else. Maybe a jacket potato."

"Did Sammy have any?"

"No, luckily. I made him a cheese omelette."

I smile and then shake my head playfully. "What's the point of watching all those bloody cooking shows if you can't even cook a chicken?"

"Very funny," she sarcastically replies. "Just get yourself a shower and scrub that stink off you. Otherwise, there'll definitely be no action for *you* tonight."

I smile. "*Action*. Well maybe I don't *want* sex, anyway."

"Yeah, right," Anna says under her breath.

But oddly enough, and probably for the first time in years, I don't care either way. I feel completely shattered—from my throbbing head, down to my blistered feet. But I'm not exactly going to turn down sex.

Seize every opportunity. That's what Granddad used to say.

* * *

I'm lying in bed, texting Wayne about the transport arrangements for the airport. I was put in charge of the minibus. *Me.* Of all people. The same person who forgot to book the honeymoon suite for my own wedding. The guy who didn't fill up the tank to drive his wife to hospital to give birth.

More fool them.

Anna is still in the bathroom—vomiting loudly. And she has been for at least twenty minutes. I try to block out the horrid retching noises by turning the TV up ever so slightly. Loud enough to block out the splashing sound of chunks hitting the bowl, but quiet enough not to wake up Sammy.

After a few minutes, I hear the noise of rushing water as Anna flushes the toilet. She then returns to the bedroom.

She looks terrible. Reddened eyes; sweat dripping down her forehead; her long brown hair stuck to the sides of her face; skin like The Incredible Hulk. She's most certainly seen better days—which is a slight relief seeing as sex is now completely off the table.

"Bloody chicken," she says, as she crawls into bed, sinking deep into the mattress and groaning. "Do you think you should sleep in the spare room tonight? Just in case? Don't fancy spewing on you in my sleep."

I shake my head. "Don't be silly. I'll be fine." I kiss the top of her head. "Just don't breathe on me when we're having sex tonight."

"Very funny," Anna groggily replies; too drained even to smile. "At least I haven't got work tomorrow. And if I'm still rough maybe your mother can watch Sammy for a few hours."

"Yeah. Just give her a ring. I'm not working 'til one anyway." I turn to face the other way to go to sleep. "Good night, babe. Just give me a shout if you need anything."

"Okay, Hun. Love you."

"Love you, too."

As I lie there, too exhausted even to sleep, all I can think about, all that races through my overworked mind is: *Please don't be pregnant. Please don't be pregnant. Please don't be pregnant...*

2

The toast pops just as another text comes through. This is now the seventh I've received in less than ten minutes. And all from the same impatient idiot: Stuart Rees. My boss.

I mean what's the rush? The delivery isn't exactly going anywhere.

"Hi, Hun," I say, as Anna enters the kitchen, holding Sammy in her arms. She sits him down in his chair, stroking his arm as she walks away.

"Hi, handsome," I tell Sammy, kissing the top of his velvet forehead. "Did you sleep all right?"

"Yes, Daddy," he replies, his voice chirpy despite it being so early.

"Did Mammy read you a nice story last night?"

Sammy just nods, beaming.

"Which one was it?"

"Nelson the Teddy Bear."

"Oh, really? That's my *favourite* one. Maybe I can read you one tonight. And when I get back from work we'll have another look for Susie. I'm sure she's just found a really good hiding place and she's just waiting for us to find her."

"Okay, Daddy."

I kiss him again and then ruffle his blond hair.

"How are you feeling this morning?" I ask Anna. "Still feel sick?

Anna walks over to Sammy and places down a small bowl of cornflakes on the table. "Yeah. And drained."

"I'm not surprised. Are you gonna be okay looking after Sammy this morning?"

"Yeah, of course," she replies, yawning loudly. "But I thought you were off 'til one?"

I pull out the two slices of toast and start to butter them. "Had a text this morning to come in early. There's been another problem in Swindon."

"Another? *Jesus.* Isn't that like the third this year? I thought they'd sorted it."

I shrug. "Obviously not. And now I've got to go in because Rich is still off with stress. I mean seriously. *Stress.* Everyone's off with stress these days. It's like the new *get-out-of-jail-free-card.* When my Dad worked down the mine, they'd have laughed right in your face if someone were off because of stress. Absolutely pathetic."

"Well, that's what you get for working in a place like Romkirk."

"Yeah, well, if we all stopped work because of a little stress, the country would come to a standstill. It's not fair to everyone else."

I take a big bite of toast, leave the other one on the worktop, and grab my jacket from the back of the chair. "Right, I better get going. You take it easy today. Nothing strenuous now."

"Yes, yes," Anna replies, as she pours herself a coffee. "And make sure you get something to eat today. Put your foot down. Otherwise there'll be nothing left of you to love."

"All right," I reply, grinning tightly. "I promise. I'll get a sandwich from the vending machine."

"Make sure you do. Can't have you looking *too* slim for Vegas. Not with all those loose women on the prowl."

I kiss her on the lips, and then playfully squeeze her ass. "You know you're the only loose woman for me. Plus, you still owe me S. E. X."

She smiles. "Don't worry, I haven't forgotten.

Now get going or you'll hit traffic."

I walk over to Sammy, slipping my jacket on at the same time. "I'll be home later to read you a story. All right, handsome?"

"Okay, Daddy. See you later."

"Love you both," I say as I leave the house.

Outside, the sun is beaming but there's still a chill in the air. I shelter my eyes with my hand as I reach the car. Winter. Typical. The one day when it's not raining, and I have to work.

I climb into my car and drive off down the street, eyes scanning for the bloody dog.

Stupid mutt. I don't even like them. I never have. But no, he wanted a dog. Not a budgie, or a fish; not even a bloody hamster. No, it had to be a great big Alsatian.

A pug would have been something.

Just a few metres before Rose Avenue, I see one of my neighbours, the soaring six-foot-three Janet Webber, standing on the pavement, getting ready to cross the road. Every time I clap eyes on the woman, I feel inadequate about my meagre five-foot-nine stature. Wouldn't fancy being married to that one. Way too tall. *And* at least forty-five. She seems to be in a trance, wearing just a white dressing-gown and blue slippers. Lazy cow. How hard is it to throw on a pair of jeans and a jacket?

For Christ's sake. What's the world coming to?

Maybe she's seen the dog.

All of a sudden she starts to cross right in front of me.

I slam on the breaks, missing her by mere inches.

"*Shit!*" I shout in fright. The noise of tyres scraping against the tar snaps her out of her daze. She holds a trembling hand over her chest as she stares at me through the windscreen.

I push the button on the door to open the window. "You all right, Janet?" I ask her. "You nearly got yourself *killed.*"

She doesn't answer.

"You all right, Janet?" I ask again. "Do you need some help?"

She then gives a smile and says, "I'm fine thanks, Rob. Just half asleep. I'll be all right." She gives a quick wave and continues crossing the road to her house.

Frowning in confusion, I return a wave and then close the window.

"Weird woman," I say under my breath as I drive off.

Whole street's full of them.

3

The smell coming from the room is enough to make anyone puke up their breakfast. But me, I'm used to it. It's almost like becoming accustomed to the smell of your own baby's nappies.

It's amazing what humans will adapt to.

Slipping the apron over my head, I catch a glimpse of Stuart through the metal-gridded window. I put on my elbow-high gloves and watch as he enters the room—that smug look on his face; those eyes too close together, almost becoming one like a Cyclops, and those short, stumpy legs and bald head. Classic *Napoléon Complex*. He's followed closely behind by two rather chunky-looking deliverymen.

"Just push them next to the wall," Stuart says, a tone of arrogance in his voice. "And be careful."

"Yeah, we know what we're doing, mate," one of the deliverymen replies. "We've been at this for twelve years."

Ignoring his comment, Stuart scribbles something down on his clipboard. "There's another sixteen outside, Robert," he tells me, not even looking in my direction. "Shouldn't take you too long. And make sure you sign off all the IL3 Forms. We can't have any mistakes with the inspection coming up. For both our sakes."

Forcing a polite smile, I take the clipboard from him and glance at the inventory. "Any details, Stu? I mean, any idea how this happened? Again?"

"Sorry, Robert, you know I know as much as you do. We get the call, and then we deal with it." He makes his way towards the exit. "Ignorance is bliss, Robert. I'll see you later. Be careful now. We don't want another incident like last week. Can't have everyone taking time off for stress." He's a dick, but I can't argue with that.

And then he's gone.

I see the two deliverymen roll their eyes at him as they wheel in the next stretcher.

No 'thanks' again for coming in early. *Typical.* I don't know why I bother. Why can't I be like the rest of the country and make up some excuse involving my baby? Why don't *I* go to the bloody doctor and complain about 'stress' like everyone else?

Because you're a grafter, that's why. You're better than that. Better than those lazy bastards.

I spend the next twenty-five minutes helping the men offload the remaining stretchers from the truck.

Seventeen. Not too bad.

The truck noisily starts up and then pulls off towards the gates.

Returning to the room, I lock the door behind me. I approach the first stretcher, and the yellow tarpaulin bag that's strapped firmly to the top. I grab a pair of safety-goggles from the shelf and slip them over my eyes, then cover my mouth and nose with a plastic mask. I carefully unzip the bag a few inches down to see its contents.

It's another child.

My stomach turns as I pull the zip down a little further to confirm.

It is. The third this month. A girl. No more than seven years old. Easily.

Any death is sad—no matter what age. But children? Never children. Children should be out riding their bikes, or playing on their computers, or whatever the hell kids do these days. Not crammed in a body bag!

It's not right.

I walk up to the control panel, turn the dial to green, and then flip the main switch. There's a loud rumble as the furnace ignites. Instantly, I can feel the heat radiate from the sides of its heavy door. The noise circulates the room causing the metal stretches to roll and rattle into each other.

Time to get to work.

Before I wheel the body over to the furnace, I stop to take another look. One last look before someone's child is reduced to nothing more than cinders. I can't help but think of Sammy back at home. I try not to. *God knows I try.* But how could I not think of him? I'm a Dad. That's what Dads do: we worry. That's what we're best at. It's not providing for them; it's not even protecting them— it's worrying about them every second of every bloody day.

And that's just sad. It really is.

Opening the furnace door, a gust of eyebrow-singeing heat hits me in the face. Despite the goggles, I close my eyes and wipe the beads of sweat from my forehead. I pull out the steel platform from inside, unclip the two straps that hold the body bag in place, and then roll her onto it. When I slide the platform back in, it feels light. *Too light.* I slam the door shut and lock it. Shoving away any lasting attachment to the nameless child, I press the large red button, and the furnace comes alive with fire, burning the body bag and its contents in a matter of seconds.

One down. Sixteen to go.

The next body bag seems a lot more filled-out, which gives me a quiet relief. I unzip the bag and see the face of a middle-aged man, with blond, slightly receding hair. I'm not supposed to open the bags. It's not my job to know—or care for that matter. But something in me always tells me to. I'm not really sure why. Perhaps it's out of respect. Or maybe just honest-to-God nosiness. Regardless, I have to look. Anna thinks I'm mad. She says that my job would be a lot easier if I just treated the inventory like inventory—and not human beings.

Maybe she's right. She usually is.

I stare at the man's pale complexion, his red, swollen eyelids, and wonder what he did for a living—when he was...living. Was he a doctor? No, he doesn't seem the type; his bright yellow shirt is too loud and way too scruffy. Maybe a vet? Possibly. Or perhaps he was just a bum like the other twenty percent of the country.

Suddenly his eyes spring open.

I flinch. And then swiftly zip up the bag.

I wheel the stretcher over to the furnace, ignoring the muffled cries through the thick plastic. The intense heat hits me again as I open the door. I slide his body inside and lock it. Pushing the large red button once again, I hear the muffled cries become a crackling sound as the body bag ignites.

Two down. Fifteen to go.

I see that the next bag has started moving already. I pause for a moment and contemplate skipping the face-check.

But I can't resist.

Unzipping the bag, I see the face of another man, this time he's a lot older, maybe sixty, and he's completely bald. His grey, deadened eyes are wide open, and I can hear faint growls behind the leather muzzle wrapped around his mouth and chin, buckled tightly around this head and neck. I wonder what he's thinking. If at all he does think. I'm sure he does. If that's a positive thing, the jury's still out, but either way, after all these years I still think of them as people. Or something similar anyway. But they're Necs. Well, that's what we call them. They're not classed as human anymore, so I suppose we have to call them something. Can't exactly call them just *The Dead*. That would only confuse them with the *actual* Dead. And we definitely couldn't refer to them as bloody *zombies*. Not only is that extremely insensitive—particularly to the families who might have lost someone to the disease—but how utterly *ridiculous* it would sound if a newsreader had to say the word *zombie* live on TV. Not a bloody chance. And Necro-Morbus Sufferer is quite a mouthful to say. So calling them *Necs* is probably the safest option. Easier on the tongue. And there's no cure, no vaccine. They've come close though, managed to put together an antiviral shot to take after infection.

But that only works a fraction of the time—and that's if you catch it early. But I suppose it's better than nothing. The government even tried to issue homes with an emergency shot, but there were just too many paranoid people, injecting themselves after any sickness: flu, food poisoning, chickenpox—even after a night on the bloody booze. It just got too expensive, so they scrapped it after about a year. Now you have to get one at the hospital.

I still wonder what's behind the lifeless eyes. I can't help it. I know it would make my job a hell of a lot easier if I didn't. But that's just me: I'm an optimist. I always have been. Even when the first outbreak happened in Swansea, I believed that these people could somehow be cured; that they were still human underneath all the decay and God-awful stench of rotting flesh.

But they're dead. I know that now. It's taken me a while, but I do.

And the dead must be burnt.

It's a dirty job. But someone's got to do it.

I reach the twelfth body and look at the time on the wall clock. 2:44 p.m. Not bad. With a bit of luck, I'll be home in time for dinner. And I'm starving to death. No lunch break again. Typical. It would be nice if once—just once—Stuart would cover me for even ten lousy minutes, just long enough for a quick bite. But no. He's tucked away in his nice cosy office, far from the trenches, sipping his herbal tea with a dash of cinnamon.

What a dickhead!

This next body bag is *definitely* not one to open. I've made that mistake on more than one occasion, and it's not something I plan doing any time soon. It's what we like to call: Moving Meat. The body bag is filled with several small bags, each one with a variety of severed limbs, everything from dismembered arms and legs to heads and torsos. Very disturbing—even for a job like this. But it's not the sight of such horrors that's so nauseating…it's the wriggling. I mean, Jesus, these things are hard to kill—not even a pickaxe to the head can bring one of these bastards down. It'll probably slow them down, but that's about it. If they can't be sedated with a tranquiliser to the head, then they're cut up into pieces and shipped. And that's the point where you have to disassociate them from human beings. You have to—otherwise you're *bound* to lose it.

The next body is a woman, mid-twenties, slim. Completely naked. Was she asleep when she was bitten or was she, in fact, a stripper, in the middle of giving some lucky guy a lap dance? I mean, she's got the body for it—or *had* the body for it. And if you look past the muzzle, grey eyes, and bloody gouge on her shoulder, she's not that bad to look at.

Guilt washes over me as I spend a little too long gaping at her slender body. She stares back at me, with eyes that no longer blink. I know she's dead and it's wrong, but I am human after all. I mean, can doctors really switch off their basic urges when they have to examine a beautiful, naked woman? I'm not so sure. And this one seems a lot livelier than the others—which makes her seem all the more alive. I check the buckle on the muzzle; it's secure. Thank

4

As I finish up the last remaining bodies, I daydream about Vegas. The lights, the booze—that's about it really. It's a stag weekend, after all. Can't see me and the guys visiting the Grand Canyon or sitting through a Celine Dion concert. No bloody chance. There'll be no time. Maybe next year, if I take Anna there. I can totally see her dragging me to some shit show, or on a sight-seeing trip. All the boring stuff. Although, I'm not really much of a gambler myself. Never have been. More of a watcher. Gambling's a little too stressful for me. Oh, I'll probably have a flutter, just to say I have, but other than that I'd rather hold on to my cash—not that I have much of that these days.

I slide the seventeenth body into the furnace and push the large red button. A sense of satisfaction washes over me as the blaze inside obliterates the old man.

Done. Simple.

The life of a Burner.

I push the empty stretchers against each other

neatly, and begin to remove my apron. Just as I'm about to hang it up on the wall-hook, I hear the bleeping sound of the code being entered outside. The door opens and in walks Stuart again. "We've got another four for you, Robert," he tells me. He's wearing his coat and holding a briefcase, clearly about to leave for the day. All right for some.

"Just four?"

"Yes. It shouldn't take too long—even for you. Just think yourself lucky you're not stuck in a stuffy office all day. I know where *I'd* rather be."

"You should try it some time, Stuart," I say through gritted teeth. "You might find it harder than you think."

"No, it's all right, Robert, I'll leave it to the Burners. Someone's got to hold the fort back there. Romkirk won't run itself." He throws me one of his smug grins. "Well, I'm leaving for the day now, so you're on your own. Call head office if there are any major problems, and don't forget to finish your paperwork."

"No worries, Stuart," I reply, forcing an obedient smile as I watch him leave.

Good riddance, asshole.

Sighing, I look at the time: 4:17 p.m. There goes another early finish.

I can dream, can't I?

When the four stretchers are safely inside, I lock the door. Slipping my apron back over my head, I think of Vegas again, and start to count the days in my head. I can almost taste the first beer in the hotel lobby. Somehow it tastes better than any other I've had. I notice that the first body bag is large. I feel relieved as I unzip it. It's a woman, no older than twenty-five, and she's chubby. Probably bullied in school. Battled with various quick-fix diets for most of her short life. Had a string of failed relationships. Classic fatty. She stares deep into my eyes. Her eyes seem sad.

I zip up the bag and burn her in the furnace.

The second body bag is small—not child-small though. This one seems another lively one. I contemplate avoiding the face-check but can't resist, ignoring my earlier near-miss. I slowly unzip the bag, and then stop to make sure that there's a muzzle strapped on. There is. Thank God. I continue to pull the zip down to chest height.

It's another woman.

My heart almost stops as I stumble backwards.

Not you.

Please God, not you, Anna.

Choking on my own breath, I creep forward. *Please let it be a mistake.* I pull down my mask and throw off the safety-goggles.

It's not a mistake.

Anna snarls behind the muzzle someone has strapped over her mouth.

I pull the zip down almost all the way.

She squirms and twists, trying to break free from the plastic cable-ties fastened to her limbs.

I can barely stand. My knees almost buckle, but I grab hold of the stretcher. I think of Sammy and wonder where he is—if he's also in one of these body bags. A frantic burst of energy hits me and I rush over to the other two. I pull the zip down on the first: it's another woman, mid-forties. *Jesus Christ,* it's the woman who lives across from our house. Susan Price. I feel sick. My heart is pounding hard against my chest. I'm sweating profusely. I unzip the last bag. *Please, God don't let it be him. I beg you.*

It's a man, early-fifties.

I thank God for that at least.

Let him be safe. Please.

Anna is now writhing so much that her stretcher has begun to move away from the wall. As I walk over to her, I think of her vomiting last night. How could I have been so stupid—so blind? I should have taken her to the hospital. They could have given her a shot. There might still have been time to save her. Was I too tired to think straight? Was I too preoccupied with a stupid Vegas trip? *Jesus Christ.* What about Sammy?

I can't seem to focus anymore. I think I'm gonna pass out. To see her like this is too much. I contemplate zipping her body bag back up. Out of sight, out of mind.

But how could I? I love her. So much. More than anything in the world. And she gave me Sammy: the single greatest achievement of my life.

I lurch over to the stool and sit. My stomach is in knots as I listen to her cries of pain and anger. I can't look anymore. It hurts too much to see her like that; a shadow of her beautiful self—her tender, placid self.

It's not you, Anna. It can't be.

It's someone else.

Please let it be someone else.

Anyone but you…

5

Another day. Another dollar.

It's a dirty job.

But someone's got to do it.

Please don't let it be me.

The three remaining body bags are now moving quite violently. Anna's even more so.

Why is her bag moving so much? Why not my neighbour's bag? Or the fat woman's? Why Anna's? Is it just pure coincidence, or is it something more? Maybe she recognises me. Maybe she's trying to speak to me? I mean, after all, they do say that each infected is different. Depending on the host. Some bite. Some don't. Others can barely move. *Christ*, some can even run!

And what if she's not dead? Perhaps they made a mistake. A horrible mistake.

Jesus fucking Christ, what the hell do I do?

As each question floods my overcharged mind, I fear for Sammy's safety. Every second spent sitting here I waste precious time. I have to deal with this. Now.

I get up off the chair and make my way over to Anna. I stare down at her face. Her eyes are empty, and her skin is drained of all life. I sprint over to the side of the furnace and vomit.

I stand, with one hand on the wall, staring down at the puddle of bile on the floor. I try to get my breath back as I wipe my mouth with my sleeve. Straightening, I take in a lung full of air and then walk back over to her. The growls from behind the muzzle disturb me like nothing before, and I can see the deadened veins in her neck pulsate as she struggles with her restraints. My eyes are fixed on hers. I can't help it. I can't seem to look anywhere else.

But I have to. For Sammy's sake.

Gingerly, I reach down and start to unbuckle the muzzle, hands shaking uncontrollably. I know it's stupid. I know she's dead. But I have to. Just to be sure. I pull the muzzle away from her mouth, dragging a web-like trail of saliva and blood in the process. I fight hard not to vomit again. Throwing it on the floor in disgust, I hear Anna's teeth clack together. The sound goes through me causing me to clench up in repulse. "Anna?" I say. "Can you hear me? It's me. It's Robert."

She doesn't respond. Just the snarls of a rabid dog.

"Anna," I say again. "It's your husband. It's Robert. Can you understand me?"

Her levels of aggression have increased as she snaps her teeth at me. The other three body bags are now moving far more fiercely—as if feeding off Anna's rage. I try to ignore it and focus on the task at hand. "Anna. *Please. It's Robert.* I'm begging you. *Please.* It's your husband. Can you hear me?"

Please…

I start to cry. I can't hold it in any longer. I haven't cried in years. Maybe a tear or two when Sammy was—

I have to get to him.

He's out there somewhere. Dead or alive, I have to find him.

For Anna.

I zip up her body bag, trying not to make eye contact, and then wheel her over to the furnace. I try not to cry, but tears are now streaming. Reaching for the door handle, I pause, only for a moment, before something inside orders me to pull it open, and to slide out the platform. I feel the heat even more so without my mask and goggles, almost unbearable. The muffled snarls from inside the body bag are like a rusty blade to the heart. It's too much. It's all too much. This can't be happening.

Not to me.

Someone else instead.

Suddenly, I hear the snapping sound of Anna's restraints. The thick plastic bag starts to bubble up hysterically, like an animal caught in a net. I quickly roll her onto the platform, barely able to see through the tears. I slide her body inside and slam the door shut.

Hand trembling, I push the large red button, and the furnace ignites. Dropping to my knees in anguish, I hold my hands over my ears to block out Anna's screams.

Forgive me.

I'm sorry.

I'm so sorry, Anna.

I love you.

6

I punch in the door-code, leaving the three remaining bodies still inside the furnace room. They'll be safe enough. No time to burn them. I race down the corridor to get to my car, ignoring the staff I pass on the way. A few even say something to me, but nothing registers. Nothing matters now.

Only Sammy.

As I approach the exit, I see the security guard. He looks at me oddly as I bolt towards the glass doors.

"Everything all right, Mr. Stephenson?"

"Everything's fine," I reply, struggling to speak as I slow for the doors. "Just late for something."

"All right. Well, you have a nice evening then."

"Thanks." And then I'm out through the doors and into the cold, winter night. I reach into my pocket and pull out my phone. No signal. *Shit!* I frantically scramble into the car, start up the engine, and then pull away, wheels squealing painfully. I speed a little further down the road and hear the sound of a text coming through. Holding the phone up against the steering wheel, I read the text:

hi hun.
hope ur ok.
will u b home 4 food?
ive made a stew
luv Anna xxx

I fight off another bout of tears as I picture Anna in the furnace room; her contorted face; the screams of agony from the fire.

Exhaling, I hear another delayed text come through:

hi hun
not feeling 2 good
cant seem 2 shift this food poisoning
going 2 ask ur mum if shell have Sammy
luv Anna xxx

I hit the steering wheel in anger, causing the car to swerve on the country road. "Fuck!" Then another text comes through. I almost don't want to read it. But I have to. For Sammy. I need to know where he is. If he's safe with Mum. I push the button and the text opens:

im sorry hun

i fucked up

i dont know what 2 do

i think im infected

come home now

Another text comes through:

answer ur fucking phone u cunt

where r u

i cant fucking

i cant

there burning

i cant see him

hun

sammy

sammy

X

No more come through.

I dial Anna's number. It's a long shot, but maybe Sammy has Anna's phone, or Mum, or anyone who can help me. Even a neighbour.

It goes straight to voicemail.

"Fuck!" I hit the steering wheel again.

I try once more, but still nothing.

I call Mum's house.

No answer.

I try Mum's mobile instead. She's never got her bloody phone on, and it pisses me off. What's the point of having a fucking phone if it's never on? Surely today of all days will be an exception. I dial the number and wait for the call to go through.

"For Christ's sake, Mum!" I launch the phone onto the passenger seat when I hear Mum's irritating voicemail message. "What the hell's wrong with her? *Shit!*" Frustration causes me to speed up even more.

The country roads are blind. Luckily I haven't seen a car since leaving Romkirk. And some of the roads have only enough room for one car. And I know *exactly* which car is getting through. Manners are out the window tonight. Nothing's going to stop me getting home.

A few miles down the road, I come to a busy junction. Cars whiz past as I try to edge out to join the main road. Can't just pull out recklessly. I'm no good to anyone dead and buried in metal. I have to be smart. Finally, I pull off to a deafening beeping sound as I almost hit an oncoming lorry. Normally I'd hold up an apologetic hand.

But not tonight.

As I race down the same old roads I travel every day, I can't help but notice the people walking by, chatting, or driving, mouthing the words to some lame song on the radio. Normally these things wouldn't register; wouldn't bother me in the slightest. I'd be too busy thinking about Vegas, or singing along to my own shit songs on the radio. But tonight, every smile I see, every calm stroll, every dog-walker, every lit up living room, just makes my blood boil. Why are all these people so content, so composed? Why aren't they running for the hills, or running to their loved ones? Why aren't they petrified like I am? Petrified that some corpse isn't out there somewhere taking bites out of their children?

Why has only *my* world been pulled out from under me?

It's not *fucking fair!*

I see a police car about half a mile or so ahead. I contemplate stopping, asking them for help. But what the hell can they do? They can't exactly get me there any faster. And if my whole street's been quarantined, there's no way they'd let some average cop through the barriers. *I* stand more of a chance than they would. Afraid they'll stop me for speeding, I start to slow down as I near the car. Can't have that. Not tonight. Have to be smart about this. No room for error. The clock's ticking.

As I cautiously pass the parked police car, I notice the two male cops inside laughing at something.

Laughing?

How could they laugh? How could they be so cold, so relaxed, when Sammy's out there somewhere? Without his father to protect him?

Without his mother.

I start to feel nauseous again as Anna's grey, deadened eyes pop into my head. I shake the image off and focus on the road ahead. The cops are now out of range, so I put my foot down again; engine screaming violently as I hit another batch of country roads.

About six miles further along, I leave the countryside and hit Bristol town centre. The pavements are packed with people. Student night. It had to be tonight. Of all nights. I'm forced to slow down as I approach a build up of taxis, cars and buses. I feel the stress start to flood my body as I almost have to stop the car because of the traffic. "*Fuck*. Got no time for this shit. Move your fucking cars! For Christ's sake!" I hit the steering wheel again in anger, and then hold down the horn. The ear-piercing noise does nothing apart from cause the entire pavement of students to stare. Normally any scene where I'm the centre of attention causes me to clench up and hide. But not now. I couldn't care less about these people. They're nothing to me. In fact, if it wasn't for this stupid black cab in front, they'd be a blur in the corner of my eye.

A minute or so passes and I'm finally through. I slam down the accelerator pedal and the car screams past the lights and out of the city centre. Still I worry about being pulled over by the police. Can't let anything slow me down. But I wouldn't let them stop me.

Not tonight.

They'll have to catch me first. Not that I'd get that far in this four-door piece of shit. I wanted the black BMW, or the silver Audi, but no, she wanted the...

Family car.

Exhaling forcefully, I hold back another barrage of tears.

I'll cry later. When I know Sammy's safe.

She's always been the boss; always got her way. And always managed to convince me that it was my way. But I didn't care. Even if sometimes I'd act otherwise. Everyone needs a leader—even if you're too stubborn to admit it.

And she was our leader. Our captain.

That's why I need her now more than ever.

Don't think I can do this alone.

I start to cry. I can hardly see the road through the tears. Tears that I promised myself I'd hold in.

Tears that I could do without.

"Shit!" I shout as I wipe them away with a sleeve. "Get a grip! Think of Sammy! You've got no *time* for this shit! *Focus!*"

* * *

Approaching Rose Avenue, I see just two police cars parked up, lights still flashing on top. I can't see any barricades, no Cleaner vans, which means two things: the infection here isn't too bad, maybe just a few isolated incidents, or they've finished decontaminating the area already—which is exactly what I don't want.

I slow down as I turn the corner for Rose Avenue. I slam the brakes on as I'm met with a storm of police vehicles, and plain white vans. But more unsettling is the fifteen-foot-high steel wall, spread across the entire junction; a portable barricade on wheels to stop anything getting out.

A female officer gets out of a police car and marches up to my window, carrying a clipboard under her arm. My stomach churns as I push the button to open the window.

"Sir, I'm afraid you'll have to turn your car around," she informs me, "and head back the way you came. You need to follow the yellow diversion signs behind you. They'll take you back into the city centre, and then down through Clifton."

"My name is Robert Stephenson, and I live on 63 Marbleview Street." I feel my entire body tremble, as I brace for her to tell me something terrible, something earth shattering—like Sammy is dead.

No! Don't even think like that! He's fine! He just needs his father—now more than ever.

The officer leans in closer to speak. "I'm afraid…" I can feel myself about to be sick again, even though my stomach is empty. I can feel my vision start to blur. I think I'm going to pass out. I can barely make out the rest of her sentence.

But then her words seep through.

"…The whole of Crandale's been evacuated.

Richmond Street, Rose Avenue, The Mount, Davies Street, and I'm afraid Marbleview too. There's been a breakout of Necro-Morbus in your area. That's all I can tell you, Mr Stephenson. Now if you can stay with a friend or a family member, then—"

"I work for Romkirk Limited," I interrupt, showing her my ID badge. "As a Burner. And I know about the outbreak. I just need to get through."

"Mr Stephenson, I'm afraid I can't let anyone through tonight. I know you're concerned, but I assure you we're doing everything we can to get your street decontaminated. You should be able to get home within the next forty-eight hours. We were lucky," she smiles, "they've managed to contain it."

Lucky? I feel my heart sink to the floor as I think of Anna. How can she say such a thing? She wouldn't think it was so *lucky* if she'd just burned her husband in a bloody furnace.

"What happened to my son? His name is Samuel Stephenson. *Please*. I haven't heard from him. Did he get out safely?"

She consults the clipboard, running her finger

down the list. I watch nervously as she flicks through each sheet of paper, my body tightening with every page she flips over. The sound is torturous. I have to massage the temples of my head to stay calm. She gets to the end of the seventh page and then pauses. She glances at me for a split second before she lifts an eighth sheet. This time the paper is red.

Red.

My heart almost stops as I watch the officer anxiously scan the page.

I know exactly what the red sheet is for. I wish I didn't. *God*, I wish I didn't. But I do.

It's the list of the infected. The dead list.

Red is for dead.

7

"How can he be missing?" I snap. "He's only four years old. There's got to be a mistake with the list. Check again. *Please.*"

The officer shakes her head. "I'm sorry, Sir; he's down as 'missing'. I'm sure he's fine. You just need to let the clean-up crew do their jobs, and then—"

"Look, if my son's still in there somewhere, then I need to get in. I need to find him. He might be in danger."

She shakes her head again, putting the clipboard back under her arm. "I'm sorry, Sir, but that's just not possible. You'll have to wait like everyone else."

"Look, like I said, I work for Romkirk. Do you know what we do over there?"

"Of course I do."

"Then surely you can let me through. *Come on*, this is what I do for a living. I deal with shit like this every day. *Please.* I'm begging you."

"I understand your concerns for your son, but there's nothing I can do. My hands are tied. And if you work at Romkirk, you should already know the procedure. So, again, I'm afraid you'll have to stay calm and wait. He's not the only one missing. There are still some people unaccounted for. And like any one of these operations, especially an area this populated, they usually turn up somewhere, completely fine. You have to be patient. Just find a safe place to stay for the rest of the evening and sit tight. The Cleaners are still searching each house. You need to give them a chance to do their jobs." She pulls a small card from her coat pocket and hands it to me. "Here," she says, "This is the number for Disease Control. Give them a call in the morning; they'll be able to keep you up to date. Okay, Mr. Stephenson?"

Okay? It's far from bloody okay. But what choice do I have? There's no way I'm talking my way in tonight. It might as well be Fort Knox.

"Where are all my neighbours?" I ask (one last throw of the dice). "Can I talk to them? Maybe someone knows something."

"I'm afraid they're with Disease Control."

"Well, where's that? Can I go there?"

She shakes her head. "No, I'm sorry, Sir, that

location is strictly confidential."

"All right, but can I just get a message to my neighbour. Just a quick question. Just a phone call or something. *Anything.*"

"I'm sorry, but—"

"For fuck's sake! Can't you do anything? I'm not asking for much, just a little help getting my boy out safely!"

"Sir, you need to calm down, please."

"No, I won't calm down! You have no idea the day I've had! No *fucking* idea at all! The shit I've had to do! And all I'm asking for is a simple phone call! One fucking phone call! It's not a lot to ask!"

A second male officer steps out of the police car and makes his way towards us. The female officer holds out a hand and her colleague stops in his tracks. "Everything all right?" he asks her.

"Everything's fine, Doug," she calmly replies, "Just give us a second."

The male officer pauses for a moment, and then gives a subtle nod and heads back to his police car.

My knuckles are white from squeezing the steering wheel so hard. I can barely catch my breath from sheer anger. I just need to punch someone; punch some*thing*. *Anything*. The frustration is too much—too much to take. I have to get through the barricade. I have to find him. I know he's in there somewhere. I know he's hiding under his bed, waiting for his Daddy to come and rescue him.

I let go of the wheel and place a hand over my chest. I feel sick again, lightheaded.

And then something occurs to me.

Mum!

"Is my mother on the list? Susan Stephenson."

Despite having almost no patience left for me, she grabs her clipboard again and reluctantly checks the list. After running her finger down each page, including the red one, she shakes her head. "She's not down on the list, Sir. What's your mother's address?"

"She doesn't live here. But she may have been here today."

The officer smiles. "Then go to her. Give her a call. She may have your little boy safe at her house. There's nothing you can do from here."

"All right," I say, as I put the car in reverse.

"Thanks."

"No problem. And good luck. I'm sure your son is fine."

I swing the car around and head towards Clifton. I grab my phone from the passenger seat and dial Mum's house. The dial tone irritates me as I fretfully wait.

"*Come on. Come on. Pick up.*"

Nothing.

I throw the phone on the passenger seat again and hit the steering wheel.

Disappointment washes over me as I drive to her house. It's only a fifteen-minute journey. I can probably do it in ten. I have to check at least. And then I'll find a way through the barricades. There's always a way in. How much would they notice someone trying to get in? Who in their right mind would want to break *into* a quarantined street? No one. No one would be that dumb.

The hard part is keeping them all in.

Suddenly my phone comes alive with blue light. Frantically reaching for the phone, I swerve the car, almost hitting the curb.

I check the display.

It reads: *Mum Home.*

I gasp in relief. Slamming on the brakes, the car screeches to a halt at the side of a deserted, industrial road. I push the accept button and hold it to my ear, hands shaking with apprehension. "Mum?" I say.

"Hi, Robert," she answers, chirpily. "Sorry I missed your call. I was in the bathroom. What's up, my love?"

"Has Anna been in contact with you today?" I ask urgently. "Is Sammy with you?"

"No. I haven't spoken to them since the weekend," she replies. Her cheery tone suddenly disappears. "Why? What's wrong?"

My phone suddenly weighs a ton as my arm just falls from my ear. Dropping my head into my palm, I start to sob. I can't help it, I can't hold it in. I hear Mum's muffled voice from the phone, but can't make out the words. Not that it would matter. She already knows that something earth-shattering has happened. Only devastation would bring me to tears in front of her.

I have to put my emotions to one side if I'm ever going to get him back. So I wipe away the tears, take a breath, and try to compose myself. Holding the phone back up to my ear, I speak—speak the words no husband should ever have to speak.

"Anna's dead, Mum."

The phone goes silent.

After a few seconds, I hear the faint sound of Mum crying. The sound is almost too much to endure. "Mum? Are you all right?"

"No. You're lying, Robert," she struggles to say, her voice drowning in desolation and shock. "Please tell me you're lying."

"I'm sorry, Mum. It's true."

"*How?*"

I brace before I answer, knowing full well how she's going to react to the truth. But I can't lie to her. I owe her that much at least. "She got bitten, Mum."

"Bitten? By what?"

I brace again. "*Bitten.*"

"Oh, my God. It's a mistake. Please Robert—it must be. *Please*. Not that. *Not that.*"

"I'm sorry, Mum."

"Tell me she didn't turn, Robert."

I don't answer.

"Tell me she didn't turn into one of those *monsters.*"

"I'm sorry, Mum. There was nothing anyone could do."

"Oh, Jesus Christ…*Jesus Christ!* What happened? Who bit her?"

"I don't know. I don't know anything. All I know is that she was sick last night before we went to bed. And that's it. We thought it was just food poisoning. She seemed fine this morning. That's why it didn't even cross my *mind* for her to go to the doctor's to get a shot. But then I left for work and…" I can't tell her the whole truth. I can't tell her what I did to her. She'd never understand— never look at me in the same way again. It's too much. This is *my* burden. *My* wretched secret. "…early today, I got a phone call, telling me about Anna."

I can hear the faint sound of whimpering. And it kills me inside. Hearing Mum in such a state brings me to tears every time. When Dad died, the only time I did finally cry was when I saw Mum break down. There's something heart-wrenching about seeing a strong person, who never lets anything get to them, crumble right in front of your eyes.

"So who has Sammy?" she asks.

A shudder runs through my entire body; crippling me. I almost want to lie to her and say he's sitting right next to me, smiling happily as if nothing bad could *ever* happen to him. But I can't. I couldn't keep something like this from her even if I tried. And I need her to help me find him.

Running a tired hand through my hair, I sigh loudly, preparing to answer. "He's still missing."

"Oh, Jesus Christ. *Jesus Christ.* Not Sammy."

"Look, Mum, try not to panic. I'm sure he's fine. I'm positive Anna made sure he was safe before—"

"Before 'what', Robert? Before she got infected? Before she turned into one of those *monsters?*"

"Mum, don't say things like that. She didn't turn into a monster."

"Then what *else* would you call it, Robert?"

"She was dead before any *monster* took over her

body. If she had even an ounce of humanity left, she would have got Sammy to safety. I just know it."

"Oh you do, do you?"

"Yes, as a matter of fact I do. In fact, I'm a bloody *expert* on the subject—seeing as I burn the dead for a living. The disease would've made her sick at first, and then she may have had hallucinations, and then it would have killed her. And that could have taken hours, maybe even days. Who *knows*. Every case is different. Everyone's body responds differently. But what I do know—what I know with every part of my *soul*—is that Anna's priority, even when all hope was lost, would have been to protect Sammy from any danger—and that includes danger from herself. And I'd put my *life* on it! And so should you, Mum."

I wait as Mum quietly processes everything that I've told her. I can feel her pain, her suffering, even through the silence.

"I know that, Robert," she weeps, "I know she would never intentionally hurt Sammy, but—"

"'But' nothing, Mum. He's safe. I know he is. And he needs me."

"So where the hell is he then? Where do you think she would have left him? With a friend? Or a neighbour? Or maybe a policeman?"

"I don't know. Hopefully one of those."

"Then what's the delay? Why don't you just *look* for him?"

"It's not as easy as that. The whole of Crandale's been infected. Everywhere from my street all the way up to Richmond. It's gonna take another two or three days to finish cleaning it. Maybe longer."

"So why can't you just say that you work for Romkirk? Get them to let you in?"

"It's no good, Mum. It doesn't matter where I work. This is the government. Once an area gets infected, they step in. Romkirk is just a contractor. They're not run by the government. And it's not the only furnace in Britain. Flashing my security badge won't mean shit to these people."

"Then what are we going to do? Wait? Wait 'til someone finds him, or worse, finds him and decides to take a bite out of him? No bloody way! You find a way in there, Robert, and you find our Sammy. And you get him out. You get him bloody out.

Tonight."

"Don't worry, Mum—that's *exactly* what I intend to do. And there's no barricade on this earth that can stop me getting to him."

8

I spend the next thirty minutes calling 'round, making sure that Anna hadn't already got Sammy out of Crandale.

No such luck.

And every painful minute that I lose just tears me up inside. I want to scream but I have to keep my head. I want to cry but I'm all cried out. I want to ram my car straight through the barricade but I'd get arrested. And what good would that do? If Sammy's still alive, then I have to get him out, and fast. Have to keep cool. Can't do anything stupid.

I'm parked up near Rose Avenue, staring at the steel wall. There are four police cars parked, and two unmarked white vans, most likely Cleaners, dotted around the area.

Absolutely no way in.

Crandale has about four, possibly five ways in: here at Rose Avenue, the turning by the primary school, and one by Richmond, plus several lanes, gardens. And I'll have to assume that every single one of those ways through will have a barricade.

These people aren't idiots. Crandale doesn't have any forests or parks, so it should have taken them a matter of minutes to stop anything getting in and out.

How the fuck am I supposed to get in?

Think.

The sewers!

A sudden wave of enthusiasm hits me—and just as swiftly it vanishes when I realise that these sewers are just a series of pipes. And even if there were sewers big enough to walk through, even crawl through, I doubt that the police would have forgotten to block them off.

Think.

Dropping my head back against the seat, I close my eyes. Come on, Rob, you're not stupid. There's always a way. Always a solution. It's not the bloody White House, it's Crandale. Just a few streets. Of course there's a way in. If you can't get through the barricade, and you can't go down into the sewers, you can go…

Up.

Opening my eyes, I see the large new houses in

front of me, just on Rose Avenue. The walls are high, but not impossible to scale. Maybe twelve feet. If I can get over without anyone seeing me, then I should be able to garden-hop all the way home. Easy.

I open the glove compartment and rummage about for a weapon. Anything hard or sharp; a screwdriver, a spanner. No knives. Definitely no knives. Not after the police put out a zero-tolerance order. Once people got wind of Necro-Morbus, everyone started carrying weapons. Knives, baseball bats—even guns. Christ, my own mother had a bloody penknife in her handbag. But like always, people abused it. Mainly the gangs from the shitty neighbourhoods, using any excuse to carry something. So now, anyone caught with so much as a slingshot will get their asses thrown in jail. I climb out of the car and walk 'round to the boot. Opening it, I see that it's bare apart from a small wheel-jack and an empty fuel can. The jack is too heavy and awkward to take as a weapon, and the metal bar is fixed on tight. *Useless.*

I angrily slam the boot shut and head towards

Rose Avenue, staying close to the walls, out of sight. Stopping at a gate, I realise how idiotic this idea is. I'm rushing. Not thinking methodically. I should at least check out the other barricades. Maybe there's an easier way in, one that's not so secure. Extremely doubtful, but still worth checking. Their eyes are on Crandale. No one's going to be itching to get in. All they care about is keeping the Necs from spreading any further into Bristol. Some stupid Dad on a daredevil mission is hardly going to be at the top of their priorities.

On foot, I make my way behind Rose Avenue. Maybe one of the back lanes is poorly guarded. But as I try to turn up the hill towards them, I see yet another assortment of flashing blue lights and vans. No steel wall though, but at least fifteen riot police, armed with shields and batons, blocking the narrow lane that leads onto The Mount.

Shaking my head in frustration, I keep walking until I'm on Crow Street, just off from Rose Avenue. There are no police. Relief washes over me as my walk turns into a jog, heading for Richmond.

After the half-mile ascent, I reach the quiet

street of Stevenage Crescent. It's a dead-end private road. Sitting down on one of the garden walls, I catch my breath. I scan the deserted street, trying to come up with a better plan of action, instead of running around aimlessly.

All right, let's think logically: if I do manage to get in, then what am I likely to come across? What sort of conditions?

Firstly, the Cleaners would've probably cleared the uninfected out, house by house, one by one, and then sent them over to Disease Control, during which time they would have started to hunt down the infected before they turned. Any already turned, they would have taken them down with a tranquillizer gun, strapped a muzzle on, and secured their limbs. If that didn't stop them, they'd have to dismember the body and bag it up—then ship it off for burning.

Or would they?

An area this big, they'd probably sedate them, gag them, and then store them somewhere in the infected zone, most likely the primary school. Or perhaps the community centre behind Marbleview.

72

Yeah. Just the right size. And easy to contain.

Gag 'em 'n bag 'em.

Turning my head, I notice that all the houses behind me are terraces. No easy access through into the gardens. I scan the rest of the row. The same. And every house is in total darkness—which could mean that this street was evacuated earlier today. But there's no police blockade. Maybe they just cleared everyone out as a precaution. *They must have.* Or maybe everyone's sleeping. No, it's way too early. What the hell's the time anyway? Reaching into my pocket, I feel around for my phone to check the clock. Empty. I check the other pocket. "*Shit.*" I left it in the bloody car!

Should I go back for it?

No!

Forget about the bloody phone! There's no time!

The entire row of houses has front porches. Easy enough to scale. Climbing into number thirteen's front garden, I carefully make my way over to the porch; one eye on the climb ahead, the other on the bay window. *Stay dark for Christ's sake.* Reaching the porch, I jump up, trying to grab hold of the ledge. It's too high. I try again. And again, until I finally pick up one of the large plant pots from the side of the lawn, and place it directly under the ledge. Destroying the plant as I step up onto the pot, I reach out and grasp the wall for balance. I tilt my head back and then leap up; the plant pot tips over as I manage to grip the ledge. My shoulders strain as I pull myself up, using my feet against the wall for a better footing. Standing erect on the porch, I gauge the main roof's height. *I suddenly feel queasy.* I quickly crouch down. Can't remember the last time I was up so high. Forgot how petrifying it is. I take a few deep breaths and try to reach up to the roof guttering. My fingertips are merely inches away, so I take another giant leap up, grasping it with both hands. The hard plastic starts to buckle from my weight, so I pull myself up promptly. I throw my legs over and I'm on the tiled roof. I stay low as I catch my breath, trying desperately not to look down. After gathering myself, I start to crawl to the peak of the roof, heading towards the chimney. I reach it, as quietly as possible, still unsure if anyone is home or not. Feeling a little dizzy again,

I grasp the chimney tightly.

What the hell are you doing, Rob?

I scan the area. In the distance, I see the flashing blue lights of Richmond's barricade. Down below, I see a row of gardens. Deserted. None of the gardens have back entrances, only high wooden fences. Directly ahead, I see the back of All Saints church. The old grey building is just a few metres from where the back garden rows end. It's surrounded by a mountain of overgrown brambles, about twelve-foot-high, making it extremely difficult to gain access.

But not impossible.

Maybe a way into Crandale?

I start to creep tentatively down the other side of the roof, heading for the glass conservatory below. Sweat running down my face, I nervously make my descent, fully conscious that one slip and I'm gone. Reaching the guttering, I carefully lower myself onto the conservatory roof. The surface appears to be extremely slippery, so I place my feet on the plastic frames separating each pane of glass. I squat and take hold of the plastic, and then spider-walk down to the ledge. Gripping the ledge, I lower my body, and then drop into the back garden with a loud thud. I glimpse at the windows in a panic; the house is still in darkness.

After noticing a light motion sensor above the backdoor, I decide to stay close to the fence, keeping out of the sensor's range. The garden has a well-maintained lawn with a small stone path running down the centre. At the very bottom of the garden, about twenty-five metres away, I see a small wooden shed. I slink towards it.

Thank God they don't have a dog.

Resting flat on the floor, next to the shed, is a small ladder, no more than seven or eight feet in length. I pick it up and carry it over to the back fence. I rest the ladder up against the fence and start to climb.

Suddenly the entire garden comes alive with light.

"*Shit*," I say through my teeth, clenching up in fright. Turning my head to the garden, I expect to see the homeowner branding a shotgun.

I don't.

Thank God.

Why the hell would I? This is Bristol for Christ's sake. It's not some dumb movie, set in some run down Texas farmyard. I scurry up the remaining few steps, and then jump down onto the overgrown grass on the other side, slipping on my ass as I land. Getting up off the moist grass, I quickly check out the surrounding area for any police or Cleaners. When I see that the area is clear, I reach up and grab the top of the ladder. Tugging hard on the top step, it lifts up, so I drag it over the fence and onto the floor. I pick the ladder up and carry it under my arm, and then make my way towards All Saints Church, my feet getting caught up in the jungle of long grass and spiky weeds.

I can't say that I've ever set foot in this church. In fact, I'm not even sure if it still *is* a church. It's always seemed so overgrown with brambles and weeds, and the graveyard is so broken and neglected, that there can't possibly be anyone working in there. Either that or the vicar's a lazy bastard.

There is a large, rundown fence buried deep in

thick brambles and nettles, too vast for anyone to crawl through, and too high for anyone to scale, even with a ladder. At the back of the church there is a tiny window, about fifteen feet up. Probably locked. I inspect the surrounding area for something to smash it with: rock, a piece of metal, anything hard. Walking a few metres along the church, I spot an old, rusty child's bike—small enough to pick up and throw, and big enough to smash the glass. I carry it back over to the window, take in a couple of preparation breaths, and then launch it up at the window. It hits the wall hard, missing the window completely. It bounces off in my direction, so I jump out of its way.

"Come on, Rob."

I pick up the bike again and take another shot. This time it strikes the window, smashing the glass. I smile in gratification, almost forgetting about what's happened today, and what horrors I'm probably going to encounter on the other side.

I position the ladder tight up against the brambles. I push hard so that the ladder makes contact with the wall. But it's no use; they're too thick. I climb up onto the first few steps and my weight manages to move the ladder onto the wall. Just. Climbing the ladder, I feel the thorny stems plucking at my clothes; the horrid nettles brushing past me. Can't remember the last time I got stung by nettles. Probably aged ten, playing in Granddad's back garden. The ladder wobbles as I reach the summit. The window is still a few metres up, just shy from grabbing distance. I bend my legs, and then propel myself up. As I take hold of the thin ledge, I hear the sound of the ladder falling away from the wall. Cautiously turning my head, I see that the ladder has plunged deep into the brambles. "Shit!" Using my feet against the wall, I manage to pull myself up onto the ledge. I crawl through the window, avoiding the small, yet razor-sharp shards of glass that are still attached to the window frame.

Exhausted, I drop into the darkness and onto a hard wooden floor; the noise echoes around the derelict church.

I can't believe I'm in. I'm through the barricades.

Back home. Back in Crandale.

As I stand in the dusty old room, a sudden wash of dread creeps over me.

I've just broken into a quarantined area where the dead are alive and well, and are probably feeding on some poor bastard as I speak.

There's a good reason those barricades are up.

9

Damp, dusty and dark.

That's probably why I never go to church—that and the fact that I don't believe in God.

How could anyone with all the shit that goes on?

I used to, when I was young. I used to be paranoid about going to Hell, about facing the Devil himself and burning for my sins. Of course, my sins were a little less significant back then. The odd stolen chocolate bar, or a few pounds from Mum's purse, or the occasional cheating on exams. Not exactly crimes of the century.

Not like burning people for a living.

The last time I set foot in a church was when Anna and I tied the knot. No, I tell a lie: it was to pay the bill for the ceremony.

Nothing's free in this life. Not even God.

I didn't really want to get married in a church. Didn't see the point. But Anna insisted. She said that it wouldn't feel like a real wedding until she walked down a *real* aisle, and said our vows with a *real* vicar, under a *real* cross. Of course, it wasn't worth arguing about it. A wedding's a wedding. Not that it made a difference when it came to signing that registry book.

And a piss up's a piss up. They say the groom can never get drunk at his own wedding—well, I managed to prove *them* wrong. So did Anna. Too drunk even to remember consummating the marriage. Not that it matters these days, anyway. Try before you buy, that's what I say.

Anna's always believed in God. Even with everything that she saw on the news. Soldiers coming home in body bags. Children getting abused and murdered around the world. Floods and earthquakes wiping out whole cities. The dead walking around, eating innocent people, spreading their disease with every bite. Even *after* all that shit, after all the pain and suffering that goes on every day, she still hung on to the belief that somewhere out there, someone was watching over her. I always told her that the only one watching over her was me.

Fat lot of good I was.

If he *is* real, then where the hell was he when she was bitten—when she turned into one of these *things?*

I try to shake off these bitter feelings of anger and remorse as my eyes start to adjust to the darkness. I can just about make out that I'm standing in an office of some sort. There's a desk with a chair on its back, and over to the left there's a large cupboard. Its doors are wide open, as if someone has ransacked it to see if there was anything of value inside. I doubt it. Maybe stacks of cash the vicar was hoarding. Apart from that, almost certainly junk.

I creep towards a door directly ahead. Each footstep on the hard wooden floor makes a loud creaking sound. I tighten up for fear of being heard. But I'm pretty sure this place is completely abandoned. Cleaners may have given it the once over as a precaution, but that's about it. Reaching the door, I grasp the handle and pull. Stiffly, the door opens. I can hear the rust from the ancient hinges rain over the floor. I step out into a passageway. There is a narrow spiral staircase at the end, just a couple of metres away. It's still almost pitch-black, apart from a small light seeping through the stain-glass window to the side. Cautiously, I make my way down the staircase, one step at a time, holding onto the stone wall all the way down. Normally, I'd be terrified of spiders in a place like this, but tonight, all I care about is getting home, to Sammy. Nothing else matters.

At the bottom of the stairs, I see a small wooden door. I grab the doorknob and turn it. Nothing happens. I push and pull it hard, but it still won't budge. I try again. Still nothing.

"Shit." I decide to kick it open, praying that it doesn't draw any attention from the Cleaners. Stepping back, I pick a spot just above the handle as if lining up a shot in a darts game. I take a breath to ready myself, raise my right knee up past my waist, and then drive my foot into the door. The noise echoes around the entire church; dust falls all around me, into my eyes. But it's all for nothing. The door still hasn't shifted. I try again, this time stepping back even further. Taking in another three preparation breaths, I line up another shot. I step forward, and then slam my foot into the door. Once again the sound carries around the building. But this time I hear the wood from the door split. I take another stab at kicking it open. And another. Then another, until finally the door is hanging from its hinges, with the wooden frame in tatters. Exhausted, I place one hand on the wall to rest. The door is still not completely open, so I barge through it with my shoulder. Breaking the door down leaves me strangely satisfied, like a cop on some American TV show.

I skulk down another dark corridor leading to a small door. There is a faint light glowing from its edges. Can't see a lock, just a handle. I take hold of the handle and push. The door is stiff, but it opens, dragging against the stone floor.

Suddenly I'm inside a huge nave, lit only by the streetlights coming through the stain-glass windows. As I step forward towards the aisle, I'm overcome with a rancid odour.

The stench of death.

And then I freeze in absolute, inconvincible horror.

A room once used as a place of worship and forgiveness, for weddings and christenings, is now bursting with at least a hundred Necs—their reanimated, rotting bodies scattered around the massive room.

Terrified beyond belief, I slowly backtrack towards the corridor. I feel my legs begin to buckle as I creep back towards the stairs, trying to remain completely silent.

Reaching the third step, something dawns on me. Why aren't the Necs storming through that doorway right now, tearing chunks out of my skin with their teeth? The noise from kicking the door would have surely disturbed them.

Something's not right.

And then it hits me: the best place to store the Necs before sending them off to the furnace is not the community centre—it's in an old, abandoned church. It's big, sheltered and has little to no chance of anyone living in it, or even in the vicinity. It's perfect.

Jesus Christ, how could I have been so stupid? So careless?

I stop about halfway up the stairs; heart still pounding; sweat dripping down into my eyes. Think, Rob. *Think*. If they're here then logically they should be secured, ready for bagging. Wrists and ankles fixed. Mouths muzzled.

I have to forcefully shake off thoughts of Anna in that way, like a nasty taste in my mouth.

If I'm right, then it should be safe enough to get past them and out the main doors. In theory, anyway. Walking carefully back down the stairs, my hands begin to tremble. When I reach the bottom, I make my way slowly through the corridor, tiptoeing silently, fists clenched. I peer inside the nave again, hoping that maybe my eyes have played a trick on me, and I've exaggerated the amount of Necs.

I haven't.

In fact, I'm sure there could even be more than a hundred dotted around the room. Next to the far wall is a row of about twenty Necs, already sealed in yellow body bags, while others, without bags, have been left on the floor of the aisle and beyond, squirming like a tank of cockroaches. But the most disturbing of all are the ones sat on the long wooden pews either side of the aisle, resembling nothing more than everyday churchgoers.

Judging by the sheer numbers, and my ridiculously loud entrance, I'm pretty sure that every single one of them is bound and gagged—otherwise there'd be nothing left of me. Even if one happened to be untied, they'd be through this door, snapping at me in a matter of seconds. So all I've got to do is walk past them slowly and then get the hell out.

Simple.

I take one slow step out into the nave, as if warily putting my bare foot into a bath of hot water. I scan the room. I was right: from what little light the church has, the Necs seem to be all muzzled-up, wrists and ankles tied. Taking slow, controlled breaths, I take another step forward past the wooden podium, and then another, and before I know it I'm standing in the aisle, ankle deep in bodies. I try not to look at them, at their eyes, for fear of an uproar. Even after all the years working at Romkirk, I've never been around so many at once. Yeah, I may have had the odd fifty, sixty bodies in one day, especially after the stadium incident. But this many—never. As if walking across a minefield, I try not to touch any with my feet as I make my way towards the main entrance. But it's impossible. I can't help but brush past a few wriggling bodies. The feeling sends a shiver of fear and revulsion through me, like walking through a spider's web. Even though my eyes are solely fixed on the double doors directly ahead, I can't help notice that some of the Necs, particularly the ones seated on pews either side, are fully aware of my presence. I can hear their stifled cries of fury from behind the muzzles. I start to pick up the pace, my feet and ankles rubbing past more and more. But it seems that the news of my arrival has begun to spread, because the room is now filled with diluted snarls and the sound of thrashing bodies. Still trying to remain calm, I speed up even more, stepping on one or two in the process. I see some of the seated Necs fall off the pews as they hysterically try to squirm towards me.

The room is now alive with movement. My careful footsteps have turned into giant leaps as I hear that horrid sound of growling from the floor around my feet. Ignoring the eruption of noise and movement filling the room, I keep pushing forward towards the entrance.

Something grabs my left ankle.

I fall to the floor onto one of the Necs; face to face, staring deep into its grey, emotionless eyes. Panic washes over me as I try to scramble to my feet. But all I can do is fall once again onto my side, in between another body. Something still has a hold of me.

Turning my head, I see a hand gripping my leg so hard I can feel its coldness through my trousers. I kick hard, trying desperately to free my leg. But it's no use. And now I can feel its other decayed hand on my right ankle. I kick out even harder, this time freeing both legs and kicking its head in the process. The Nec rolls away onto its side as I quickly get to my feet. I jump over the last few bodies and watch in loathing as it slithers like a python towards me, mouth still gagged, ankles still bound. Struggling to catch my breath, I bolt towards the entrance, knowing full well that it's only a matter of time before more of them break free of their restraints.

Slaloming past one or two more Necs, I manage

to reach the entrance, not looking back once, not even when I hear the sound of another restraint snapping. Just as I'm about to grasp the door handle, I pause for a moment. Expecting the door to be locked tighter than a bank vault, I find that it's slightly ajar. Confused, I give the huge door a nudge to open it. As it slowly opens, I catch a glimpse of a Cleaner. Male. He's lying on his back on the concrete paving, wearing his thick, white clothing and black gloves. His riot helmet is on the ground next to him, its thick, plastic visor split down the centre.

And crouching over him, tearing into his throat like a lion would over a gazelle, are two rotten Necs, fighting for flesh.

I almost consider returning to the nave, back to the swarm of bodies. But I can barely move. I feel my limbs start to seize up as I watch in absolute disgust as the man is eaten in front of my very eyes. I can only pray that he was dead before they got to him.

But that's unlikely.

I manage to somehow move slightly forward,

hoping to find a safe path to make a run for it, before the Necs notice me. But as I look down the side of the church, towards the overgrown graveyard, I see another Cleaner being ripped to shreds by four other Necs; half his face and scalp devoured; his glove and fingers missing. This time one of the creatures sees me. With a mouthful of blood-soaked hair and torn skin, he growls at me, his ravenous eyes locked firmly onto mine. Then a female Nec, which has her back to me, slowly turns her head towards me, her jaw also dripping with blood.

I freeze again, eyes fixed on the Nec as if face-to-face with a wild animal.

Do I run, or do I keep still?

Either way, someone has completely fucked up this so-called clean-up operation.

10

Fight or flight.

A concept that, until now, has never raised its ugly head. Even back at school I managed to avoid any real confrontation. But this, this is a completely different level of fight or flight. This one has teeth, riddled with disease, an uncontrollable violence seeping from its pores, a raging hunger for human flesh—and, of course, this one is as dead as a doornail!

Quickly scanning for all my possible exits, I feel my body return to life from its frozen state. I see a rusty gate, which leads down onto Richmond.

Suddenly I burst into a sprint, kamikazing down through the overgrown graveyard, around the four Necs. Can't look back. Have to ignore the strained screams I can hear behind me. Getting closer. And closer. I focus on the gate, blocking out the thudding of footsteps ploughing down the grassy bank, just metres from me. I fight the urge to look back, to see how many are chasing me. But the impulse gets the better of me. Turning my head, I see four, maybe five Necs in pursuit. The sight is almost too much for my thrashing heart. Turning back to the gate, I see a gravestone directly in front. Too late to dodge it, I try to hurdle it instead. But as I'm nearly clear of it, my foot clips the top, propelling me into the air. I land painfully onto my side, momentum rolling me down towards the gate. Shutting out the pain, I scramble back onto my feet, but the Necs have managed to gain a few metres. One of them is close. I can smell the stench of rotten flesh as it nears.

Reaching the gate, I consider trying to leap over it, but it's too high, even with all the adrenaline surging through my body. I slam into the gate and push hard. *It's jammed!* The frantic shrieks of fury and hunger are deafening as I barge the gate as hard as I can. The gate only half-opens, but still nearly taking the hinges with it. Just as I squeeze through the gap, the first Nec is there, snarling loudly, spitting disease from her unmuzzled mouth. I grab the gate and slam it into her chest as I close it. The force knocks her down; the sound of ribs cracking echoes around the graveyard. But somehow she recovers in a second, unfazed by the effects of the heavy metal gate. I kick the gate as hard as I can to jam it shut, at least to hold them off for a few more seconds. The others are now behind the gate, clawing and barking at me, so I turn and sprint in the other direction onto Richmond. Completely exhausted.

That was close.

Too fucking close.

Not sure how long that gate will hold them back. Not long. Need to keep moving.

Nothing seems real as I tear down the deserted road, running just on fumes. Not even the familiarity of Richmond. Everything's in tunnel vision, like some strange dream. I mean, I recognise everything: the house colours, the post-box up ahead, the redundant telephone box, even the old bus stop. But at the same time it's as if I've never set foot here in my life.

I pass tens of parked cars. Not a good sign. More cars mean fewer people got out. But it could also mean absolutely nothing. After all, maybe the Cleaners just piled all the non-infected onto a bus or something, and then just drove the hell out of here. Yeah, that makes more sense. No point in thinking the worst. The church was probably just an isolated incident. Can't expect a clean-up this big be without a few stray Necs, without a few casualties. Backup is probably on its way now. The riot police are probably ready to burst in and take care of everything, to sort this bloody mess out. Not too soon, I hope; can't risk getting caught—not when I've come this far. Sammy could be just around the corner.

I *know* he's alive.

I can feel it.

Approaching the junction of Davies Street, about three hundred metres from home, I stop behind a parked car. Can't just sprint across; I'll be too exposed. The street could be littered with Cleaners and Necs. I stay low to the ground, spider-walking towards the last house before the junction. Reaching it, I slowly poke my head out to peer down the street.

I gasp in terror as I swiftly retract my head.

The entire street, road and pavements are

teaming with Necs. Seventy. Maybe even a hundred. Too hard to tell. A tidal wave of dread washes over me, fists squeezing together to stop them from shaking.

How the hell did things get so bad?

This is *not* what I imagined.

Do I just make a run for it, and hope that somehow I won't be spotted? Or do I wait it out somewhere?

No, waiting is *not* an option. If Sammy's hiding somewhere then I can't have him waiting even a minute longer than he has to. I just can't.

But what if I get caught; get bitten and turn into one of those things? Or worse still, get eaten alive? What use will I be then?

Christ! This is a nightmare. I can't believe I'm here, in my own bloody neighbourhood, petrified that someone might eat me alive. I mean, how can an ordinary day turn into something so unthinkable, so unbearable? This morning I had a wife, a future, and a four-year-old son safe in his bed.

Now all I have is a street full of walking corpses trying to kill me.

I hide behind a car while I think of my next plan of action.

Plan of action? I've done fuck-all *planning* since I left the furnace. Everything I've done has been reckless and spontaneous. It was sheer luck that Stevenage Crescent was deserted. And it was sort of lucky that I could get into the church—well, apart from all the Necs.

So, *planning* can kiss my ass! And with that, I get up, take in a deep breath, and then dart across Davies Street's junction as fast as my legs can carry me. I don't look down at the hordes of Necs. There's no one to save. Maybe any other day, any other situation, I'd stop and help, maybe drag a Nec off some poor bastard, maybe pull them to safety. But not tonight. Not while Sammy is just past this junction. Not while he's waiting for his Daddy.

Not while—

I can't bear it any longer; I have to turn to see if they're following me. Halfway down, I glance over my shoulder. Relief washes over me when I see that I'm all alone, running along the pavement.

I slow down into a fast-walk, all the while fully

aware of the looming danger all around me, in my so-called safe and perfect neighbourhood. Every inch of this once beloved place used to be somewhere me and Anna could bring Sammy. Push him up the hill in his pram, towards the school by Crandale Park.

Bliss.

Don't think I can do that again. Not now, after everything. Can't see me wanting to stay 'round here after what's become of it. Not without Anna.

We'll probably move. Somewhere away from people. Somewhere without any chance of widespread infection.

Somewhere safe.

Almost at the end of Richmond, I spot someone. A man. Well, more of a teenager. About sixteen. I stop for a moment, cautiously squatting down by a parked car. Is he alive? Too hard to tell. Can't see any blood; any bite marks. Perhaps he needs help. Or maybe he's seen Sammy.

Just as I'm about to stand and call for his attention, the teenager turns his head in my direction. I feel a sudden surge of dread when I see that half the boy's face is missing.

As he limps across the road, I can't help but feel sadness. Not terror this time. But a consuming pity for him. After all, he's a victim in all this chaos, this contamination. He's not the enemy. It's the disease that's the enemy. He's just a boy who got bitten. Nothing more.

Still crouched down like a terrified cat, I wait for the disfigured teenager to pass. I see a glimpse of his distorted face through the car's wing mirror. I hold my breath as his moans of torture pass me by. The sound eventually disappears back towards Davies Street. When I see he's out of sight, I stand and continue forward. Just a few metres down, the road starts to curve around to the left, leaving me blind to potential dangers that lie ahead.

Still keeping low, using the parked cars for cover, I creep around the corner. When I see that the coast is clear, I feel my tense body relax a little. Not too much though. Any one of these surrounding houses could have a horde of rampant Necs, just waiting to burst out and devour me.

I cross my fingers as I make my way around the

corner. Just as I see the bottom of Richmond, I spot something that stops me in my tracks. Just a metre before the junction leading onto Marbleview, I see a white van on its side. One of the Cleaner vehicles. I quickly duck down by another car and wait to make sure Necs aren't ransacking it. After a few minutes, I hear nothing, other than the noise of static coming from the radio inside. I can almost make out muffled voices buried in the crackling sound, but nothing that makes any sense.

Judging by the damage, it looks like the vehicle has lost control and hit one of the parked cars.

Any survivors? Must be. The impact doesn't seem that bad. Of course, any crash would draw attention—and the last thing you'd want to do is draw attention here.

I move closer to the van, car by car, still keeping low to the ground. Can't risk being seen by any more Necs when I'm this close to home. But I have to check out the van, make sure that there's no one still inside, injured.

Stop!

What the hell are you doing?

You don't have time for this shit! You've got to keep moving!

I peer down the street towards home, and then at the van.

I'm so close.

"*For fuck's sake,*" I mutter as a flood of guilt and curiosity hits me at once.

I approach the van from the back entrance, pissed off that I'm too weak-minded to leave well alone. The doors are both closed. When I reach them, I grasp the handles and pull.

Locked.

I walk to the front of the van, along the exposed underneath. I take a look through the front shattered windscreen.

"Jesus Christ!" I foolishly shout when I see the driver still strapped in.

It's too difficult to fully make out the driver because of the spider-web crack in the glass. All I can tell is that the driver is male. I race over to the side of the van and climb onto the door, which is now facing upwards. I tap on the window, hoping to get some kind of response from him. I don't.

Dead.

For now, anyway.

Pushing my face up to the window, I try to get a better look inside. With his face covered in blood, slumped over a deflated airbag, I hold out little hope.

Just as I'm about to climb off the van, and back onto the road, the man suddenly comes to life.

"*Shit!*"

I leap off the van, falling backwards as I hit the hard concrete. I'm about to bolt down the street to Marbleview, when I hear a faint, "*Wait,*" coming from inside the van. Now, I'd be the first to admit that there are a few things I don't know about Necro-Morbus, but talking Necs is not one of them.

I go back to the side of the van and climb up onto the door. He's facing the window, fully awake, wearing his white protective suit; his black hair shaved close to his scalp, most likely ex-army. In spite of a severely bruised face, and a shattered nose, he's very much alive. Unquestionably not a Nec. Or at least, he hasn't turned yet.

"Are you okay?" I ask, still trying to keep my

voice low.

The driver nods.

"Can you move?" I ask.

The driver shuffles in his seat. *"A little,"* I hear him struggle to say, wiping the blood away from his mouth.

I tug on the door handle, but it's stuck. "Unlock the door and I'll pull you out."

The driver nods, and then fiddles with the door handle, but nothing happens. "It won't open," the driver tells me. "It's jammed."

I give the handle another pull but the door still won't budge. "Open your window instead and I'll drag you out."

The driver presses a button on the door panel. Once again nothing happens.

"It won't open," he says.

I check to see if the keys are still in the ignition. They are. "Turn the key to get the battery on."

He takes hold of the keys and turns them. Nothing happens. "Dead," he tells me.

Poor choice of words.

"Cover your eyes and face," I say, "I'm gonna

break the glass."

The driver follows my instructions and protects his face—as if bracing for an explosion. Using my right elbow, I strike the window as hard as I can, closing my eyes tightly as it hits. The glass remains the same. Not even a scratch. Despite a searing pain shooting up from my elbow, I ready myself for another attempt. This time the window breaks, spitting shards of broken glass all over the driver. He shakes off the sharp pieces like water off a dog, pushes the seatbelt button, and then tries to move. For some reason, he can't. "What's wrong?" I ask.

"The steering wheel's buckled and jammed into me. I can't get out."

He struggles to free himself as blood continues to pour from his nostrils.

"Are you all right? You're bleeding pretty bad." I reach in to help free him.

"I'm fine," he replies, trying to move his seat back away from the steering wheel. "Just smashed my nose. Nothing serious."

"So what happened to you? Did you get attacked?"

"No, I just had to swerve to avoid some crazy woman standing in the middle of the road." He gives up on the seat adjustment and continues trying to wriggle free.

"Was she dead? I mean, well, you know what I mean—was she a Nec?"

"Fuck knows. Could have been. Hard to tell. It happened so fast. Next thing I know I've crashed into a parked car and tipped over."

"Well, you're all right now. Did you have someone with you?"

"No, just me. I was meant to pick up some colleagues when everything went tits up."

"What the hell happened here? How did things get so out of control? Normally you guys are in and out in a matter of hours."

"Usual story: fucking budget-cuts. Not enough Cleaners to detox an area this big. Things just got too much to handle. We haven't had a breakout this size since the stadium."

Finally, the driver manages to free himself from the steering wheel. I start to pull him out of the vehicle. Suddenly, I feel something ice-cold grip onto my exposed calf. I turn to see what it is.

"*Oh fuck!*" I shout as I catch sight of the Nec, grasping my leg.

Wrenching my ankle from his tight grip, I roll onto my back against the side of the van. To my horror, I see six, maybe seven Necs around the van. Looking up the road, I see maybe ten or so, on route to us. Some of them hobbling. Some are sprinting.

"Oh shit!" the driver cries. "There's too many of them! Get me the fuck out of here! *Quick!*"

I reach into the vehicle, grab the driver by his arm, and then yank as hard as I can. He yells out in pain, but I ignore it. I'm too preoccupied with the crowd of Necs, trying desperately to climb up.

I manage to pull the driver free from the van, and we are now both standing on the side of the vehicle. The other Necs have reached us. The sheer weight of their bodies, scratching at the van, causes it to shake under our feet. I grab hold of the driver to keep balance.

"Jesus Christ," I say. "What the fuck do we do now? We're surrounded."

"Don't panic," the driver replies. "We're not surrounded. They haven't got the intellect for strategy. And they can't get at us from up here either."

I back off from a mass of wrists and fingers, scrabbling against the metal by our feet. "Where's your gun?"

"It dropped down somewhere when I crashed."

"Then let's go get it then."

"Too risky," he replies, shaking his head. "We'll be cornered. We're safer up high. Only got a few rounds left anyway."

"*Shit*," I say, as the groans coming from the Necs cut through me like a squealing drill, and the smell is almost unbearable. But the terror of seeing so many, without their wrists and ankles bound, without a muzzle strapped onto their mouths is even more excruciating.

Home is so close. Just around the corner. Sammy could be there now, waiting—*terrified*.

I scan the rest of Richmond; I can't see any other threat.

The Necs have clustered just below us, so the

other side of the van is clear. "We need to get off this thing, right now," I say, stamping down on a Nec's fingers as it reaches for me. "We can make a run for it."

The driver examines my escape route and nods in agreement. "Yeah, all right." He kicks another in the face; blood sprays across the pavement. I cover my mouth in case any gets in. Not worth the risk. Nec blood is still highly contagious for about a minute in the open air.

The aggression is clearly building in the Necs as they clamour for a better reach of us. I try not to look any of them in the eye. If I do, then I start to see the person, or even the neighbour lost inside. And that makes me think of Anna. And now is not the best time to think of her.

"You ready?" the driver asks me.

"Yeah. I think so."

And with that, we both jump off the clear side of the van. I land clean, hardly losing my balance at all. Just as I start to bolt, I see the driver down on the floor, holding his ankle.

"Come on!" I scream. But before I can even

contemplate going back for him, a storm of Necs are on top of him.

As I back away, I can no longer see the driver, only the mass of vultures kneeling down, all around him, biting and tearing off chunks of his flesh with their teeth and fingernails.

I can't help him. How can I? It's too late. He's finished.

No way for a man to die. Especially when he's just doing his job.

This fucking disease.

I run down the street towards home. I know that there's nothing I can do for him. If I had a gun then maybe things could've been different. It was just bad luck. Wrong place. Wrong time. Nothing more.

Then why the hell do I feel so guilty?

Just up ahead, I see the junction to Marbleview. As my street sign comes into sight, I can't help but feel elation. But then an overwhelming sense of panic devours it. What if I find him dead? Or worse still: turned? What if he's—

Shut up, Rob! You're not helping things.

Pull yourself together. For Sammy's sake.

Reaching the junction, I stop for a moment to see if any Necs are following. Luckily they're not. Not so lucky for the nameless driver. Poor bastard. Too busy tearing him to pieces to come chasing after me.

I shake off another dose of guilt as I creep around the corner onto Marbleview. The coast seems clear for now. Although, I still keep low to the floor, using the parked cars for cover again. There's no reason to think that this street is any safer than the rest of Crandale.

Car by car, I finally reach my front door. My stomach churns at the sight. Never before have I felt so terrified of entering my own house. Mine and Anna's first house. Sammy's first home. Where he took his first steps. Where he...

Stop it! Stop torturing yourself! Just get inside. Sammy needs you.

Just a car or two down, I notice Anna's car still parked. I skulk towards it. I don't know why. Maybe to find a clue—something to point me in the right direction. Reaching it, I notice that the back passenger door is ajar. The door that Sammy uses. The knot in my stomach twists and tightens. Images of Sammy laying dead in his booster-seat fill my head. I shake them off in disgust as I slowly open the door.

The car is empty.

Thank God.

I take a quick look in the front and back of the car; almost forgetting the imminent threat that's all around me. Frowning in confusion, I close the door and sprint back to my front door.

Reaching into my jacket pocket, I feel about for my keys. A split second of dread hits me when I think I've lost them. I exhale in relief when I manage to dig them out. I push the key in the lock and turn it.

The door opens and I walk in.

11

The house seems different. Unlived in. At least for some time, anyway. As if someone had died here many years ago and it's now up for sale.

But how could it feel so different—so *strange?* This is my house. I was here just this morning. How could things change so quickly?

I'm about to reach for the light switch next to the door, when I stop suddenly just inches from it. *Think!* No lights. Can't let them know I'm in here. Too risky. Luckily, the light from the street lamp faintly illuminates most of the hallway, just enough to see in front of me.

I hold off the desperate need to call out to Sammy. I have to be sure the house is Nec-free. For all I know, Sammy could be under one of the beds, hiding, and when he hears my voice he could coming running out—straight into a pack of hungry Necs.

I listen out for noise. Any sort of noise. Rustling. Whispering. Anything.

The place is dead silent.

I need a weapon.

Scanning the front hall, I see nothing, other than a pile of Anna's umbrellas rammed into a deep vase. I grab one and pull it out. It's pink, with a flowered pattern on the handle and fabric. I inspect the tip, hoping that it's razor sharp. It isn't. It's just a scuffed piece of pointy-ish plastic. Useless. It wouldn't pierce toilet paper, let alone a Nec. Maybe I could use it as a stick.

Christ! An umbrella as a weapon? Who the hell am I supposed to be? The bloody *Penguin?*

I need something better. God, I'd kill for a gun. Any gun. Preferably a machine gun. Not that I've ever *used* a gun.

I slide the umbrella back into the vase, annoyed that I'm not better prepared for an attack.

Cautiously, I enter the living room. Luckily the door is already ajar, so I peep in before I'm inside.

Too dark to see. Just faint outlines of furniture.

Need a torch.

I walk beneath the electrical fuse box positioned by the front door. Reaching up, I manage to open it. Using just my fingertips, I feel about for a torch. I hear it roll back and forth along the wooden ledge, until finally it falls out into my other hand. I push the button. It works. Thank God for that.

I shine the torch into the living room, corner to corner.

Clear.

No sign of a struggle. No obvious blood stains, thank God.

I walk over to the couch, climb up onto my knees, and take a quick look behind it. Once again, it's clear. Relief and disappointment wash over me in unison.

Back in the hallway, I decide to check out the kitchen, leaving upstairs until last. As I enter the kitchen, I swap the torch to my left hand and hold my right fist up, ready for any surprise attacks. The room is clear. Even the dishes are done and put away. No signs of a struggle. No signs of any blood. I wipe a thick layer of sweat from my brow as I start for the back utility room.

Opening the door slowly, tightening up as I pray that the hinges don't squeak. Luckily, they don't. I shine the torch, and then poke my head through the half-open door. The room is deserted. Walking in, still on high alert, I notice that the washing hasn't been taken out of the machine yet. It was probably the last thing on Anna's mind before——

Stop it, Rob. *Focus.* You can cry later. Right now you've got a job to do.

I feel the tension start to ease when I notice that the backdoor bolt is in the locked position. I double-check the handle just in case.

I make sure that the windows in all the downstairs rooms are closed and locked.

Standing at the foot of the stairs, I suck in a huge breath of air, readying myself to take the first step. The staircase is just a standard ten to fifteen steps, but for some reason the height seems mountainous—as if reaching the summit would be some kind of great achievement.

I start the climb; each step creaks like the staircase of an old haunted mansion. Every noise ripples through the silent house, causing me to tense up even more. I increase my pace, hoping that the sound will lessen with speed. It doesn't. Halfway up, I see my bedroom door ajar. My heart is pounding hard against my chest as I complete my ascent. I'm unsure of whether I'm terrified of walking in on a horde of Necs, or discovering Sammy harmed. Probably both in equal measures.

I shine the torch. The landing is deserted. Not a single thing out of place. Every picture of Sammy is hanging, completely intact and straight. Even the vacuum cleaner is still under the small table next to the bathroom; still not put away from two days ago.

Pushing my bedroom door open, once again I clench up in anticipation to whatever horror might lie in wait. I creep inside, scanning the room quickly in case something jumps out of a corner. Not that there's an abundance of hiding places; just a double bed, a wardrobe and two bedside tables. I drop to one knee and shine the light under the bed. Empty, apart from a few of Anna's stray shoes and a box of some kind. I walk over to the wardrobe and open both doors simultaneously. Nothing but clothes, more shoes, and a stack of boxes. I close the doors and exit the bedroom.

I cross the landing and enter the bathroom. Walking in, I feel a cold breeze from the open

117

window hit me in the face. I quickly explore the room. Deserted. Thank God for that. The last thing I could bear now is to pull back the shower curtain like some horror movie, and discover something sinister lying in wait. Luckily for me, our shower is glass, and as for the rest of the bathroom—you couldn't swing a dead cat, let alone have a group of Necs crouched down in some corner.

My stomach begins to curdle when I exit the bathroom.

Next stop: Sammy's room.

I can barely walk through sheer, all-consuming dread. I hold up my fist again, as if ready to go into battle, to step inside the ring. Using my foot, I push his door open. It creaks loudly as it swings, revealing his darkened bedroom. I enter, shooting the light of the torch in various directions like bullets. His room is small, so I manage to see most of it in a second. It's empty. I walk in, feeling a terrible sadness and panic that I'm most likely not going to find him in here. I check the wardrobe. Nothing. I drop to my knees to peek under the bed. Empty, apart from a few toys. Staying on my knees, I whisper Sammy's name.

And again.

And again.

Until I'm screaming it.

Sobbing it.

I can't breathe.

Where are you, Sammy?

Please…

12

I'm in the living room, sitting on the single sofa chair, staring at the faint light coming through the closed curtains to the right. The gap separating each curtain shows me a little from the street outside. Barely. I've seen at least three figures walk past. Most likely Necs. No living person would be strolling down the road. Not tonight. Maybe yesterday.

I take another sip from the bottle of lager, and then wedge it between my thighs. Even though I'm no longer using the torch, my eyes have adjusted to the darkness. I can now make out everything in the room, not just the silhouettes of the furniture. It still doesn't feel like home. Even though I'm drinking the alcohol I purchased just last weekend. And even though I'm sitting on the cherry coloured sofa that Anna picked last year, despite us having a row over the price and colour. It's not home. Not anymore. Not without Sammy and Anna. How could it be? They were the heart of this house. Without them, it's just an empty shell. Just a building for squatters to piss in.

I can't even bring myself to look at the photos of Sammy, sprawled along the wall. It's too hard. There's also a wedding photo of Anna and me that's been burning a hole in the side of my face. I felt it from the moment I sat down.

Too much has been lost.

I gulp down the last of the lager, and then set it down on the floor. Just as I'm about to get up for another, I hear a loud stomping sound outside the front window. Frozen solid, I try to make out the noise—living or dead. But by the sounds of the snarls and cries, it's pretty clear what's out there.

Getting up from the sofa, I make my way towards the door.

Time for another drink.

Walking through the darkened hallway, into the kitchen, it's as if I can see in the dark, like a blind man. But how could I not know my way around this place? I've spent enough time here, making quick trips down to the kitchen from bed. Usually at Anna's request. Not that I minded—in spite of a little protest. She's worth any request. Anything in the world.

Even burning her in the furnace?

Shut up! Someone had to do it. I'd never let anyone else push that red button. Only me. She's *my* wife. It's *my* responsibility. *My* choice. I know with every ounce of my being that she would *never* want to live as a monster. Not in a million years. It's no different to switching off a loved one's life-support machine. It *has* to be done. Someone's got to do it. *Someone's* got to make that choice.

I'm glad it was me.

Glad I was there.

At least, if a part of her was still in there, at least I was the last face she saw.

Before she—

I wipe away a few tears from my cheeks as I open the fridge door. One lager left. Don't know why I feel disappointed. It's not like it's the worst thing to happen today. I grab the bottle, pop open the cap with the bottle-opener, and return to the living room.

I sit down on the sofa chair again. Taking a huge gulp of lager, I listen to the sounds of animals rioting outside. I place the bottle between my thighs again, and then cover my ears with my hands. The noise outside fades. I close my eyes and think of Sammy. My little boy. Where is he? Why can't I muster up the strength to find him? I made it this far. I got past the barricade. I survived the church. Why can't I think of a solution? I know he's not dead. I'm sure of it. He's alive somewhere. I *know* he is.

So why isn't he here with me?

I press harder against my ears as the screams begin to seep in. Now all I hear is an echo, like the ocean at night.

And the faint sound of a telephone ringing.

Is it my mind playing tricks on me? Am I losing it? God knows I'm due.

I slowly remove my hands from my ears. Turning my attention to the coffee table to my left, I hear the sound again.

And again.

Knocking over my bottle, I reach to answer it; terrified that the ringing will alert the Necs outside. I pick up the receiver and hold it to my ear.

I brace for a moment before whispering: "Hello?"

13

"Robert," the voice on the line whispers. "Is that you?"

"Yes," I whisper back, apprehensively, as if about to be scammed by some cold-caller. "Who's this?"

"It's Edith. Edith May. From number sixty-one."

A smile forces its way across my face. Never thought I'd be smiling tonight. Not until I find Sammy, anyway. *"Jesus,* Edith. Where are you calling from? Next door?"

"Yes. I heard you come in earlier. I wasn't sure if it was you or one of those men."

"Thank God you're all right. Is my son with you?" I ask, desperation in my voice. "Is Sammy there?"

"No. Sorry. I haven't seen him."

"What about Anna? My Wife? Have you seen her today?"

"No, I haven't. Is everything all right, Robert?"

My heart sinks.

"Can you get to me?" she asks. "From the garden? It's too dangerous from the front."

I don't answer. What's the point of going over? I'm just wasting time; she can't help me.

But what's the alternative? Raid the drinks cabinet? Sit here and get drunk, hoping that Sammy will just knock on the front door?

No! That's stupid! I'll go to her. Maybe she knows more than she's letting on. There must be something she can do to help. "Okay, Edith. I'm coming over to you. Sit tight."

"All right, Robert. But for the love of God be careful. Those things are bloody dangerous."

"I know. Don't worry now. I'll see you in a second."

"Okay. Just give a little tap on the backdoor and I'll let you in."

"No problem."

I hang up the phone and leave the living room, and then race eagerly to the utility room, despite the shortage of light. At the backdoor, I reach for the lock, but then stop all of a sudden as my fingers touch the metal latch. *Slow down. You're rushing.* You don't know what's out there. There could be a hundred of those things just waiting, ready to tear your head off.

Be smart! Be methodical!

I go to the window and pull the blinds slightly to the side to see into the garden. The small garden is way too dark to make out any Necs. I can't even see any outlines of various garden features, like the flowerbed, and the lawn, or even the shed. But I don't see any movement, so that's a plus.

I unlock the door, and then carefully start to turn the handle, as if defusing a bomb. The door quietly opens, and a gust of cold air blows into the room. I can feel the tension start to build again in my muscles as I step out into the pitch-black garden. It's silent apart from the sound of faint cries from the front of the house. Moving stealthily, I can feel the blind terror gripping my body with every step. I can just about make out Edith May's wall, but other than that I see nothing, not even moonlight. As I'm just a metre from the six-foot wall, I pray that I don't kick over a metal bucket. Not sure if I even own one. Maybe one of Sammy's *many* garden toys.

Just as I reach the wall, the sensor-light comes on, filling the garden instantly with colour.

My heart almost stops dead in fright.

There is a female Nec standing next to the shed.

She spots me immediately and darts towards me, her angry, ravenous screams echoing around the garden. It's merely a blink of an eye before she reaches me. I panic and make a dash for the wall that separates Edith and I. But there's no time to scale it. I can feel the Nec as she claws at my jacket from behind. I hear her jaws snapping together as I try to shake her off. Turning, I see her dead eyes, her lifeless skin, the bite mark on her left forearm. I manage to grab her wrists and pry her from my jacket. I'm too afraid to punch her in the mouth in case of infection, so I drive my knee into her chest and thrust her away from me as hard as I can. She flies backwards, landing on the ground. Turning to the wall again, I hear her scramble to her feet. With my back pressed hard against the wall, I slam my foot into her stomach. But this time she stays on her feet.

Need a weapon.

I quickly scan the ground for something. Anything. Something hard. Something sharp. *Where the hell's a chainsaw when you need one?* Next to my feet I notice Sammy's mini-trike. I kick the Nec again and then reach down to grab the small, metal toy. But before I can hold out any hope of swinging it, she's on me. With my jacket once again in her clutches, she pins me against the wall—her teeth just millimetres from my face. Still not wanting to drop Sammy's trike, the only barrier against her teeth is my left hand, which is firmly wrapped around her throat. Even though she hasn't breathed air for some time, I can still smell the rancid, dead breath-like odour as she angrily snarls. The stench is overpowering.

And then suddenly the garden is in darkness again as the light goes out. I can no longer see the Nec, only hear her, *feel* her…*smell* her. I don't know how far she is from biting me—all I know is that I have to get her off me—and *fast*.

I manage to lunge my right knee into her stomach, which only drives her back a little, but enough to make her release my jacket. I lift my leg up and kick her backwards. As she soars away from me, the garden light comes back on, revealing exactly where she is. She bolts at me, black bile oozing from her mouth, I swing the trike as hard as I can, smashing it into the side of her head, knocking her clean off her feet. Not wanting to take any risks, I decide that one hit isn't nearly enough. I cover my mouth from the thick spray of congealed blood, as I continuously beat the woman's head with the trike, until there's barely anything left of it.

Satisfied that the danger has gone, I step back—exhausted—and stare down at the Nec's limbs, very much alive, still clawing blindly at nothing. I drop the blood-soaked trike and make my way over to the wall. As I climb, I take another look over my shoulder at the body. Have to be sure. I've seen enough movies to know that you should never assume that they're dead—or in her case, immobilised. The word *dead* has lost all its meaning.

Can't believe I have a body, with a caved in head lying in my garden. Jesus Christ, how things can change so quickly.

At the top of Edith May's wall, I try to see

through the darkness of her garden. Don't fancy having another encounter with a Nec. From what I can remember, her garden is almost identical to mine. In fact, all the gardens on this road are the same. And so are the houses. I can't see any obvious movement, and I'm sure the noise from my previous fight would have disturbed any lurking Necs. Just to be safe, I let out a short and sharp cough. I listen out for any response. There's nothing—just the sound of the female Nec's limbs writhing behind me. I cough again. Still nothing. Then suddenly I almost fall off the wall in fright when I hear a loud squeaking sound.

Tensing up, I ready myself for round two.

"You all right, Rob?" a soft voice asks.

Relief washes over me when I see Edith's face pop out from the backdoor. "Thank God for that," I say, holding a hand over my thrashing heart. "Thought you were one of them."

"No, just me. None of those things out here. I'd know if there were because my garden light would come on. Great inventions, don't you think, Robert? They stop cats shitting on my lawn—and now they warn me if any of those bloody monsters are here too. Money well spent, I think."

"You're right. They *are* great." Then I drop down into her garden.

14

Edith guides me into her living room. The only light is coming from the landing. I pull the curtain slightly to peer into the street. There are several Necs roaming—some just sitting in doorways—while others are beating fists on front doors and windows—most likely trying to break in to feed on some poor bastard. But for all I know they could be trying to get into their own homes, some kind of sub-conscious memory left over after death.

I sit on the couch next to Edith. Her frail, pitiful body, almost hunched in her seated position, makes me wonder if she truly knows the severity of today's events. I mean, she's old, maybe seventy-five, and she seems surprisingly relaxed. But then that doesn't mean anything. People deal with stress in all sorts of ways. She's not exactly senile. Yeah, she may be a little forgetful, but who isn't. *Jesus*, I'm lucky if I can remember the names of half the people I work with. God knows what I'd be like in forty-odd years.

"I'm so glad you came over," she says, as I notice her white pyjamas bottoms tucked into her thick bed-socks. "Hope it wasn't too much bother for you."

"No bother, Edith," I reply, ignoring the memory of the garden-Nec. "I'm glad you called. How long have you been here?"

She shrugs. "Since yesterday. Well, actually, the day before. I don't really know what happened. One minute I'm outside calling for Bateman—"

"Who's Bateman?"

"My dog."

"Oh, right," I say, nodding. "I didn't know you had a dog."

"Yeah. I haven't had him long. Maybe six weeks or so. He doesn't go out much. More of a housedog. He's a little pug. He's been missing for nearly two days now. I'm shouting his name, then all of a sudden I hear loud sirens going up and down the street. And then Shirley, from five doors up, calls me. Tells me that some police officers and some men in white suits came and took her sister away, up on Richmond. And said that one of those creatures tried to break into her house. And then the phone just went dead."

"So you didn't see Sammy or Anna today? At all? Maybe leaving my house in the morning?"

"No, sorry. I didn't see much of anything. We just locked all the doors and windows, closed the curtains, and waited for the police to arrive."

"Did you see anyone with a child, maybe another neighbour?" I ask, struggling not to break down, to keep my composure. "Or a policeman? Anyone at all?"

She shakes her head disappointedly. "I'm sorry, Robert. I was too busy trying to secure the house. I don't have a burglar alarm, so I had to make sure everything was locked up tight. Never seen one of those creatures before. *Horrible things.* Before any police even knocked on my door, I could hear them outside. Screaming. A few even tried to get in. They soon gave up and moved on to the next house. Thank God. Horrifying. Absolutely horrifying."

I run my fingers through my hair and sigh loudly. "What time did this all start? What time did you hear the sirens?"

"Not sure. About ten, maybe eleven this morning.

"And the news? Have you watched it? What's it say?"

"Not much. They're saying that it's all an isolated incident. And there's nothing to worry about. But once it went dark, I had to switch the TV off. Too much light in the room. They'd know I was in here. The room lights up like a Christmas tree with that thing on." She points to the TV, which is resting on top of a wooden cabinet.

"They probably won't show everything that's happened until after they take back control. They wouldn't want any panic. And who could blame them—I wouldn't want the country to know that I couldn't sort out a few streets. I mean, Crandale's not exactly London, is it?"

"So what's happened then? Usually, these things get sorted out quickly."

"Budget-cuts. Well, that's what one of those Cleaners told me before—" I forcefully shake off visions of the driver getting eaten alive, and try to move the conversation on. "So how've you been keeping with all this going on? Have you been hurt?"

"No, I'm fine. Luckily we managed to stock up on food this morning. You never know—could be stuck in here for a few days. Not that I get out all that much with my heart the way it is. But at least we won't starve. There's enough for all of us."

"What do you mean?"

"Well, we've got enough food to last us at least a week."

I shake my head in confusion. "No, you said you went shopping this morning. I thought you said you'd been home for the past few days."

"I have."

"Then who brought you the shopping?"

"My brother."

"Oh, right. I see. And did he just drop it off to you and leave this morning?"

"No."

"Then where did he go?"

Edith tilts her head back and motions upstairs.

"I've locked him in the bathroom."

15

Peter Morgan.

All that's keeping him inside the bathroom is a red and blue scarf, with one end tied around the bathroom door handle, and the other fixed to the banister opposite. I can barely believe my eyes. How she managed to get him in without harming herself is beyond me.

Maybe she's not as frail and helpless as I first thought.

"How long's he been in there?" I whisper, shaking my head in bewilderment, staring at the door handle.

"All day," Edith replies, switching on a second lamp. "He came home with the shopping this morning. Put most of it away for me, even though he said he felt unwell. I offered to put it away myself, but he insisted. So I let him. He's a stubborn one. Always has been. I put the kettle on and then he said he felt sick. So I told him to sit down and leave the shopping alone. But, typical Peter, he never listens, he just carried on. And then he was sick. All over the kitchen floor. He then ran past me, straight up the stairs to the bathroom. I followed up after him to make sure he was all right."

"Was he bitten?" I ask, eyes still glued to the door handle, subtly listening out for any movement from inside. "Did you see any bite marks on him?"

"If he was bitten then he kept it hidden from me. That's Peter all over—too proud to admit when he's hurt."

"So what happened next?"

"Well, he was in there for a while. Vomiting loudly. I offered to call the doctor, but he said he was fine, so I went back downstairs to clean up. I thought he had a bug or something. Or food poisoning. After I cleaned the kitchen and put the rest of the shopping away, I went back up to see if he was feeling any better. When I got there, he was tying the scarf around the door handle. I couldn't understand what he was doing, but he insisted that I lock him in by tying the other end around the banister. I refused of course. I mean, it seemed ridiculous. Why on earth did he want me to do that? At worst, it might have been a bug, I thought. But then he screamed at me, demanding that I do as he says. Now we've had our disagreements in the past—but Peter's never screamed at me like that before. It was as if he was a different person. He scared me. I mean, *really* scared me. So I did what he asked and tied the scarf as tight as I could to the banister. He told me under no circumstances am I to open that door. No matter what happens." Edith shakes her head. "And I haven't."

"Look, let's go into the bedroom and talk," I say, my stomach in knots at the thought of Peter bursting through the door. Although I still haven't heard a sound. Not even a faint rustling. Maybe he's dead. *Real dead.* Not everyone comes back. Not everyone's body can take the change. He could be in there lying in a pool of his own vomit.

"There's no need to go into the bedroom," Edith says. "He can't hear us. I've knocked on that door a dozen times, and I've heard nothing. I even called his mobile phone, but it just kept ringing from inside his pocket."

I check to make sure that the scarf is still tied tight enough. "You do know what's happened to your brother, Edith? I mean, you do understand why he asked you to lock him in?"

"Well, I didn't at first—but I do now. He's infected. Or at least he *thinks* he is. And he was worried that he might turn into one of those things from outside. But I doubt it."

"Why do you doubt it?"

"Because it's Peter. He's as strong as an ox. I can't see one of those things being able to bite him."

"Listen, Edith, you may be right, but if he *has* turned, then that scarf isn't going to hold him for very long."

"Well, it's kept him in this long. And if anything, he's more likely to be passed out in there. Surely not everyone who vomits is infected. People can still get sick without it being Necro-Morbus."

"Yes, you're right. But anyone who vomits today *and* yesterday might be. Including Anna. She was sick last night too. And now she's dead."

Edith puts a hand over her mouth. "Oh no, not Anna. I'm so sorry, Robert. I didn't realise. How awful."

"It's all right. But we have to secure that door."

Walking up to the bathroom door, Edith puts an ear to it. "The thing is, Robert, there's a reason I called you over here."

"And what's that?"

"I need a favour. I want you to open the door and check on him."

I shake my head in protest, nearly laughing at the very notion of such a ludicrous thing. "What? No. Not a chance. For *your* sake as well as mine."

"*Please*, Robert. You're the only one who can. I promised him I'd keep the door locked. But I need to see if he's okay. Or at least know if he's…"

"Look, I'm sorry, Edith. I really am. And I *get* why you need me to do it—but I just can't. I'd have to be *crazy* to risk it. It doesn't matter if we haven't heard him, he still could be contagious. *And* aggressive. One bite and—"

"What if it was Anna in there?" she asks, coldly, unable to even make eye contact with me. "Or Sammy?"

Leaning against the banister, I sigh loudly, unable to believe that she would say such a thing.

But she's right. Of course I'd open the door. Of

course I'd check. I'd have to. Even if she was banging on the door. Growling. Even if—

Shit.

What a *fucking* night.

"Look," I say, sounding defeated, "even if I *did* open the door—what good would it do? Whatever we'll find isn't going to change anything. And by morning I'm sure there'll be help coming. Someone with the correct equipment can open the door. Someone with protection. I mean, if he *is* turned— and I'm only saying 'if'—but if he *is* turned then we'd be completely defenceless. We'd have to hit him with something. I mean, *really* hit him. Hard. Is that something you can handle?"

Edith begins to sob. It rips my heart out to see it. Especially someone so innocent, so good-hearted. Someone who probably hasn't hurt so much as a fly in her life.

But it's the truth. I *would* have to smash his brains in. Most likely right in front of her. Not a lot of people could cope with that. I know *I* couldn't. But I can't exactly strap a muzzle on the guy and throw him in the furnace. And no matter what

Edith may think about the many possible reasons for his puking up—I'd bet my life on it that he's infected.

"I don't care," Edith struggles to say as she wipes her eyes with a sleeve. "I have to be sure. He could be passed out on the floor, totally helpless, just waiting for someone to come."

"He also could be waiting for someone to tear limb from limb. I know it's hard to hear, but I've seen it. I've seen it with my own eyes. I've seen what this disease does to people. Innocent people. Like your brother. It just takes and takes, until there's nothing left of them. And once that happens, it's no longer them. It's no longer the person you love looking back at you. And it'll never be again. And you can't think anything less. You just have to deal with it. You just have to accept that they're gone. For good. And all that's left is this horrid, relentless illness."

Edith walks over to a wooden chest next to the bathroom door, and sits. I notice her shaking hands as she places one hand on her forehead.

"You all right, Edith?" I softly say.

She doesn't reply.

There's an uncomfortable silence that lasts for about a minute.

Until finally Edith lifts her head up to speak.

"Open the door."

16

I slip on a pair of Edith's thick, green-coloured gardening gloves, and then tuck my sleeves into them so that there's no flesh exposed. I do the same for my ankles, pulling my socks up over my trousers. I then wrap one of her pink scarves over my mouth.

I catch a glimpse of my reflection in the landing mirror and decide I look like a bloody idiot.But who cares. I'm not here to look good.

Clutching an old, scuffed-up cricket bat Edith found under the stairs, I feel every muscle tighten with dread as I watch her untie the scarf from the banister.

"You ready?" I whisper.

She nods to me when the scarf drops to the floor, still attached to the door handle.

"I need you to wait downstairs," I tell her. "It's too dangerous up here."

"No. I can't. I need to see for myself."

"Don't be stupid. I'll soon find out if he's infected, and then…"

"And then what? Bash his head in with the bat? Listen, I appreciate this more than you know. And I know you've got your own problems, Robert. But I need to see if he's still alive. And if I'm here and he *has* turned into one of those things, then I'm not going to stop you doing whatever it takes to protect yourself. But if I'm downstairs then I'd always wonder in the back of my mind if you made the right call."

I take a look around the landing. "All right. Fair point. But there's no room out here. At least get out of harm's way. Go back to the bedroom, so you can still see."

Following my instruction, she walks over to the bedroom and stands in the doorway.

I lightly tap on the door, stomach churning with nerves, and call out to him. "Peter?"

I wait for an answer.

Silence.

I knock a little harder. "Peter? Are you okay? It's Robert. I'm a friend of Edith's."

Still nothing.

I let out a long breath to ready myself, and then

reach for the door handle, my hand quivering as I make contact. Delicately, I try to twist the knob. It doesn't budge.

"He's locked it from the inside," I point out. "I can't believe I could be so *stupid*. Of *course* he did. Why the hell *wouldn't* he?

"What now?"

Staring at the door, I brace myself to do the only thing I can. And if I don't do it now, then I'll never have the balls to do it. So I drive my right foot into the door, causing the wood to splinter. I repeat the action and the door flies open. I leap back, cricket bat held tightly in my grip, ready to take Peter down.

"Do you see him?" Edith nervously whispers. "Is he all right?"

Shushing her, I creep forward towards the open bathroom. The room is dark, but the lamps from the landing give off just enough light to see. My heart is pumping fast like a racehorse as I poke my head through the doorway. Peter is nowhere to be seen. But it's only a matter of time. Inching forward, I see the toilet and sink. Still no sign of him. The anxiety is almost too much for me; beads of sweat dripping from my forehead, in spite of the cold, damp room. Edging around the door, I see the bathtub. Empty. Next to it is the shower cubical. Its frosted-glass doors are closed, and the room is still too dark to see even a silhouette. Taking one hand off the handle of the bat, I reach forward and grasp the rim of the shower door to slide it open.

"Is he okay?" I hear Edith say from directly behind me, causing me almost to swing the bat at her in fright.

"*Jesus Christ, Edith*," I snap; bat still aimed at her head. "*Get the hell out.*"

She goes back out onto the landing.

"*Shit*," I mutter to myself, still unable to shake off the shock.

Deciding against opening the shower door, I give a gentle tap on the glass. I wait for movement. A sound. Anything at all. Something to indicate what sort of a state he might be in. I hold my heavy breathing to listen.

No movement.

No sound.

Dead?

Well, old-fashioned dead.

I give another tap to the shower door, only this time a little harder. Still nothing. Putting the cricket bat between my thighs, I slide both glass doors open simultaneously. Once completely open, I secure the bat again; grip tight, ready to brandish it.

Peter Morgan.

I've never met the guy before. Didn't even know she *had* a brother. And here he is, lifeless, slumped up against the tiled shower wall, in his smart black suit; dressed as if about to attend a funeral. How fitting and tragic. Even with the room's poor lighting, I can see his thick head of hair, too thick for a man clearly just a couple of years younger than Edith. And I see his eyes shut, as if doing nothing more than taking a nap in front of the TV. But from the smell, I'd say he's been dead for most of the day. Poor bastard.

Poor Edith.

"Is he dead?" Edith whispers from the bathroom doorway.

Shrugging, I move a little closer. "I think so. And I don't think he's one of them, either." I gently prod his chest with the end of the bat to make sure. No response. "I'm sorry, Edith—but he's gone."

I can hear her weep, but I don't turn to her. I can't bear it. I know I should, but I can't. Instead, I just gawk at his dead body, as if seeing one for the very first time. In fact, the very first time that I *did* see a dead body, it was a reanimated one. I never even got to see Dad's body. Not that I really wanted to. But I *was* curious. I mean, who isn't. Everyone slows down when there's a car crash, hoping to see something nasty. It's human nature. Even if it's someone you love dearly.

"Are you all right, Edith," I ask; eyes still fixated on Peter.

All I can hear are muffled sobs from the bedroom. I'm not even sure if she heard me.

Poor woman. I think she always knew that whatever we found locked in this room wasn't going to be good news. But seeing her brother sitting up on the shower floor—*dead*—is a damn sight better than seeing him as a Nec. Anything is better than that.

No one should have to see a loved one in such a

horrid, unforgiving way.

I finally manage to turn away from him, and head for the doorway. "You all right, Edith?" I call out quietly, pulling the scarf from my mouth. I lean against the bathroom doorframe, watching her from across the landing as she sits on the side of her bed, weeping. It breaks my heart—but what can I do? I have to leave soon. Have to think of a new plan. Can't stay here all night. Sammy's out there somewhere. Most likely alone and afraid. He's already lost his mother. And for all I know he saw her turn as well. *Jesus Christ*, don't let him have seen her in such a state. At least give me that much. At least give me something.

For *fuck's* sake.

"Can I get you a glass of water?" I ask her. "Or something stronger?"

She doesn't answer, just shakes her head slowly as if in defeat—as if this was the last thing that life was going to throw at her.

What now? Do I just leave Peter's body in the shower? Or do I need to take it somewhere?

Leave it. What good would it do? And besides,

he could still be teaming with infection. Doubtful, but why risk it? Probably need to throw a sheet over him. And then keep this room closed until Crandale is properly cleaned. But fuck knows when that's gonna be. Shit, they'll probably drop a bomb on us before they let this get any more out of hand.

"I'm gonna find a sheet to put over him," I tell her. "Is that all right?"

She looks up at me, eyes bloodshot and streaming, and then smiles thinly. "That would be nice, Robert," she calmly replies. "Thank you. And I'm sorry I had to put you through all this palaver. I know it's not fair on you; you've got your own worries to see to."

I return a smile. "Don't worry about it. Let me get you a glass of water, and then I'll find a sheet. You stay put."

Walking back into the bathroom, I can't resist catching another glimpse of Peter. Poor bastard. At least he still had the sense to lock himself in. Edith doesn't know how close she came to being bitten. Or worse—ripped to shreds.

Sometimes death *is* better.

I set the cricket bat down against the bathtub, and then grab a glass from the sink. Filling it with cold water, I stare at my reflection in the mirror. This is the first time that I've stared at myself since this morning. And for some reason, I look different. Not so much from the stress and the hardship of the night's events—just *different*. But who wouldn't after burning their own wife in a furnace.

Stop it!

It wasn't your fault. You need to get past this.

I glance again at Peter as I make my way out of the bathroom.

"There you go, Edith," I say, as I hand her the water.

She takes the cup with a smile

"I'm gonna look for something to cover your brother," I say. "Do you have anything I can use?"

She takes a sip of water and then points over to the spare bedroom across the landing. "In the other bedroom," she replies. "On the wardrobe shelf. You should find some clean sheets."

Clearly putting on a brave face, she takes another sip of water, her hand still trembling. Maybe it hasn't fully sunk in yet. I mean, it's a hell of a lot to take in. For anyone. Better get that sheet before she gets a look at him. The last thing she needs to see is her dead brother sitting on a damp shower floor.

Exiting the bedroom, I head over to the spare room. Once inside, I have to stop myself from flicking the light switch on. The room is dark like the rest of the house, but I can still find my way over to the wardrobe. I try to look inside, but I can't see a thing. Reaching in, I feel about for a shelf. I can't find one. Doesn't seem to be one in here. I keep blindly rummaging for about a minute before realising that there are two wardrobes. I close the doors and open the other wardrobe, positioned right next to the first one. Inside, I feel for a shelf and find one. I locate the sheets straight away and pull them down, dropping various other pieces of clothing in the process. Just as I'm about to close the wardrobe doors, I hear the sound of glass shattering. And then a loud, piercing scream.

Dropping the sheets, I race out of the bedroom to the landing. Peter has Edith pinned to the floor of her bedroom. I reach them in a heartbeat and grab the back of his shoulders, prying him off her. He falls onto his back and she quickly scurries further into the bedroom, out of the way. Before he can get back onto his feet, I plunge my foot down into his face. Edith screams at the sight, but I have to do it. Can't let him get back up. Unaffected, apart from a split nose, Peter turns on the floor and grabs my ankle, causing me to lose balance and fall back against the banister. I cry out in agony as my lower back hits the thick wood. Peter snarls; foam dripping from his teeth; eyes almost entirely colourless. I back off slightly, terrified as he follows me towards the spare room, like a cat about to swoop on its prey. As I pass the bathroom doorway, I spot the cricket bat. In a second, I bolt inside the bathroom and grab it. I hear his violent shrieks as he chases me inside. But before he reaches me, I swing the bat recklessly, smashing the mirror above the sink. I close my eyes and flinch as shards of glass spray everywhere. I take another swing, this time catching him on the side of the head, nearly knocking him back out onto the landing. Realising that there's clearly not enough space in the bathroom, I ram the end of the bat into his face in a stabbing motion. I repeat the action until Peter is back out onto the landing. I follow him until I'm standing over him, pounding his head with the bat; unconcerned about the splashes of blood flying all over everything, including my face. I continue to swing the bat down onto his head, wave after wave, as if chopping down on a thick log with an axe; splitting his skull like firewood. I forget where I am. I forget who this is. All I feel is an uncontrollable urge to destroy him. To end his suffering. To end this consuming disease.

To…

"STOOOOOOP!"

I drop the cricket bat when I hear Edith's voice.

I can't turn to her. I can't face it. All I can see is Peter; his face no longer resembling a brother. It's now a mess of congealed blood and broken skin. Even his limbs are hardly moving.

What have I done?

I lost myself.

I forgot who I was.

How could I do that to her? She didn't deserve to see such a *vile* thing.

But what choice did I have? He was trying to kill his own sister. He would've happily killed us both. Without a second thought.

I had to.

Peter was dead even before he walked through that front door. I know it. He knew it. The only person who *didn't* know it was Edith.

Exhaling loudly, I feel my pounding heart begin to slow. I turn to face Edith. She's not crying. Not anymore. She's just standing there, eyes wide with horror, clutching her right forearm tightly.

I can see the blood seeping out between her thin fingers, running down into her other hand.

I know that look.

I've seen it before.

If only I could have seen it on Anna.

17

I'm watching the street from the living-room window. There are still several Necs loitering like teenagers in doorways and on pavements.

It's strange. From here they almost seem human. Normal. But they're not. Far from it. They're just walking disease. Death with legs.

Monsters.

Edith is still in the kitchen, trying to clean the bite. She won't let me in. She's afraid she might infect me. I told her that she doesn't have to worry—that everything will be fine.

I lied.

I don't know what to do. I have to search the street for Sammy, but I wouldn't last five minutes. And what about Edith? I can't just leave her here. She's infected. It's only a matter of time before she turns.

If only I had an antiviral shot. So what if they're hit or miss? At least she'd have a bloody chance!

How could they let this happen in the first place? How could they let it get so out of hand?

This place should have been swept in an hour. Maybe then Sammy would be safe. Not lost somewhere in a Nec-infested street.

They can clear a football stadium in an hour, so why can't they deal with this? How hard can it be? Gag 'em 'n bag 'em. Simple. Football hooligans are more dangerous than Necs.

At least with Necs they only bite.

I hear the living-room door opening behind me. Turning, I see Edith standing in the doorway, with a bandage wrapped around her forearm. I no longer see the nosy-old-cow from next door, always snooping through the window. Now I just see an elderly woman, broken and bloodied in her own home.

"How are you feeling?" I ask.

"I'm okay," she replies.

I give a sympathetic smile. "How's the arm? Does it hurt?"

She shakes her head. "No. Not really. Just a little sore. It's fine. You don't have to worry."

"Of course I'll worry. The last thing I want is—"

"So how long?" she asked suddenly.

"How long for what?"

"How long do I have before I turn into one of those things?"

I'm shocked that she's so blunt with her question. But who can blame her? It's a valid question. But it's one I thought she might avoid asking. Or at least delay.

I almost tell her that nothing's going to happen to her; that it's not deep enough to spread the infection.

But instead I say, "Not long."

She nods, as if accepting of her fate with just those two words.

"Everyone's different," I add. "Some last days before—" I can hardly bring myself to say the words. But I do. "—Before it kills them. Some just hours. It depends on the person; how strong they are. How deep the bite."

"So I'm guessing a seventy-six-year-old doesn't stand much of a fight then? What, hours?"

I run my hand through my hair and sigh. "Probably."

"Okay. I can live with that."

"What do you mean you can *live with that?*"

"Exactly what I say. I'll do what my brother did and lock myself in the bathroom."

I can't believe how calm and collected she seems. I know I'd be climbing the walls, probably sawing off my arm with the kitchen knife. Not planning to barricade myself in the bathroom and waiting to die. "Are you sure that's such a good idea? I mean—"

"Then what's the alternative? Suicide?" She shakes her head in repulse. "Not a chance in hell. I'd never give in like that. Not without a fight. I don't believe in suicide. Never have done. And I don't intend starting tonight."

"I wasn't saying suicide. But when the infection reaches your brain, you'll come back as one of those *things*. And you might hurt someone. *Anyone.* Someone you love. And then you'll have to be put down. But it won't be something quick like a bullet to the head. Bullets don't work. They'll come for you, stick a muzzle over your mouth, stuff you in a body bag, and then some asshole will throw you in a furnace and watch you burn. Yeah, you'll be long gone. You'd have died long before you could hurt anyone—but is that how you want your body to be treated? Nothing more than walking disease? I mean, Edith, I'm against suicide as well, but sometimes—"

"Sometimes you just wanna go out the way you want to. We don't always get a choice. But at least *I* do. And this is *my* choice."

I shake my head, unable to comprehend her words. "But it's *not* a choice. You'll end up *killing* someone. Spreading the virus. Is that what you want? I know *I* wouldn't. And I know damn well Anna didn't want that either. That's why I did what I did. That's why I burnt her in the furnace. And I'd do it again in a heartbeat! She would've done the same for me."

Edith sits on the sofa chair as she takes it all in. She seems exhausted, drained of spirit. But it's no surprise. She's just lost her brother—and she's infected.

Jesus Christ, this is a fucked up night.

"What do you mean 'you burnt her'? What—

alive?"

"No. Well, not exactly. She was turned. *Long* turned. And my job is to burn any Necs. No matter who they are. I work for a company called Romkirk Ltd. We get Necs shipped over to us from across the country. And we burn them in a furnace."

"Oh, my *word*. I didn't know, Robert. I thought you worked in a factory. Somewhere in town. I had no idea."

"Most people don't know. It's not a secret. It's just easier to keep it from people. Hard to explain. It's just a job. Like any job. But every day I have to burn the dead."

I can see her eyes begin to well up again. "Oh, Robert—you poor man. I can't believe they made you burn your own wife. That must have been *horrific*."

I don't answer, just nod, trying to hold off yet another bout of tears. In one hand, it's painful talking about Anna, but on the other, it feels pretty good to tell someone. Even if it is just a neighbour. A neighbour that I haven't spoken to in months. Someone that I hardly know, despite living next door to her for three years.

"It *was* horrific," I say. "But I didn't have a choice. Anna was already dead. It may have *looked* like her, but she was long gone. All I burnt in the furnace was her diseased body. Nothing more. It wasn't Sammy's mother," I point to the street behind me, "it was one of those things outside."

The room goes still. I can see Edith just staring at the window, stroking her bandaged arm. I feel terrible. I may not have intended to bring up suicide, but I didn't exactly give her any alternatives.

Edith stands up from the sofa chair, unable to make eye contact with me. "I'm going to get a glass of water. Can I get you something?"

I'm about to speak, but nothing comes out, so I just shake my head.

She exits the living room, and all I'm left with is a deep, overwhelming feeling of guilt, bubbling up in the pit of my stomach. I try to shake it off but can't. And then Sammy's face pops up in my head. I see him playing in the garden, riding on his little red trike. And then I see the Nec from the garden. Blood and brains smeared all over his beloved toy.

Edith returning with a glass of water stops an image of an infected Sammy forming.

Thank God. Can't let myself even contemplate the notion.

Never.

Edith sits back down and takes a slow sip from the glass. I notice the skin above the bandage has blackened. The infection is spreading. I try not to draw attention to it, but she spots me gawking. She looks at her arm, and then tucks it down into her side.

"I've made my mind up, Robert," she says calmly, as if about to tell me what pizza topping she's chosen. "I want you to lock me in the bathroom. Like Peter. And I want you to leave his body in there with me. It's suicide, or this—and suicide is simply not an option. Do you think you could do this for me? One last favour before you go? I know it's a lot to ask, but I've got no one else. And I'm afraid that if I *do* turn, then locking myself in won't be enough. I'll need you to secure the door from the outside too."

"I can't put you in the bathroom," I tell her,

shaking my head. "Even if I wanted to."

"Why not?"

"Because I kicked the door in. Remember?"

She nods. "That's right, you did. I forgot. Okay then, how about my bedroom then? That should be—"

Before she can finish her sentence, she gets up, cupping a hand over her mouth. I spring to my feet as well. "What's wrong?" I ask her, a tone of panic in my voice. She doesn't reply. And then she staggers quickly out of the living room. I follow her into the kitchen. Reaching the sink, she vomits loudly into it, without time even to remove a pan full of dishes.

I stand clear. Too afraid of contamination. I want to put a hand on her back for comfort but can't. Have to be careful. For Sammy.

I'm all he's got left.

After a few minutes, Edith's head emerges from the sink; eyes bloodshot; sweat pouring down her face. She wipes her mouth with her arm and groans loudly.

"Are you okay, Edith?" I ask; still standing a few

metres away. "Can I get you anything?"

She doesn't speak, just shakes her head. She then pulls out a chair from under the kitchen table and sits heavily, as if suddenly weighing a ton.

I also pull out a chair and sit. I watch her in silence as she holds her head up with her palm, clearly struggling to shake off the nausea.

It's spreading. It could be any time now. Can't see someone her age lasting too long. Have to get her locked up soon. Can't believe I even brought up suicide to her. Who the hell do I think I am? *I* wouldn't do it. So why the hell should she? And even if she *did* decide to do it: how would she do it? Gun to the head? Doubt if she's got one of those lying around? Pills? Who knows how long they'd take to kick in. It might be too late. She'll still turn. And I'm not exactly going to hack her to death with a chainsaw.

She probably doesn't have one anyway.

Ignoring my reservations, I place a sympathetic hand on her shoulder. "I think it's time, Edith. I'm sorry."

She pulls her head away from her palm, looks at

me, eyes still red, and nods. "You're right." She lets out a long breath and then smiles. "No use putting it off any longer. You've got your little boy to find."

"I didn't mean that to sound like I was rushing you. I only meant—"

Putting her hand onto mine, she smiles again. "Don't be silly, Robert. I know what you meant. You think I haven't got long. Because of the vomit. You think it's already in my blood."

I struggle to pluck out a suitable, painless reply. But all I can muster up is a subtle nod.

"Then let's get it over with," she says, standing up, focused, almost seeming optimistic. "I can listen to the radio in the bedroom anyway. Not too loud, though. Don't want them hearing it. Can't put you in any more danger." She leaves the kitchen, heading towards the stairs. I follow. "Peter and I used to love listening to the radio in bed. Not the music. Only the stories. We used to have the sound down low, you know, just in case Mum heard us. She'd get so mad with us. Of course Dad never heard us. Always too drunk."

We make our way up the stairs. I'm aware of

how loud her voice is. It's echoing around the entire house. I'm petrified that someone might hear. But I don't have the heart to tell her. Not now. Not when she's about to lock herself inside her bedroom to die. Can't do that to her.

"Sometimes," she continues, "we used to be under the sheets listening to it. Sometimes the sound was so low we had to hold an ear to each speaker. And Peter used to—" She stops when we reach the landing, and she sees Peter's legs sticking out of the bathroom. They're partly covered with the sheet, but his leather shoes are still in view.

Thank God it's too dark to see the blood over the floor and wall.

When she reaches the bathroom doorway, she looks down at her brother's covered body. It's not moving anymore—but the virus is still very much alive. I know that for sure. Racing through his dead cells; somehow hanging onto life even without the brain. Don't know how long it'll last before giving up. Days. Weeks. Who knows.

That's why the dead must be burnt.

It's the only way.

Staring down at him, she smiles, blows him a kiss, and then mouths the words: *I love you, Peter.*

She walks across the landing and into the bedroom. I follow behind, avoiding a glance at Peter as I pass him.

Inside, she sits on the bed and reaches over to her alarm clock. She picks it up and starts to turn a knob at the side. Suddenly the sound of loud static fills the room. She quickly adjusts the volume, and the sound lowers. She fiddles with the dial and the static is replaced with the sound of a man's voice.

Edith looks up at me and smiles. But this time her smile seems genuine. Not the forced smile of loss and hopelessness.

This is a smile of happiness.

She sets the radio back down on the bedside cabinet.

"I'm ready now, Robert," she says. "You can lock me in."

18

I could have gone back home. But I couldn't do it to her. Not yet. Maybe in a few minutes.

I can still hear the faint sound of the radio from behind the door. I'm not sure if she knows I've been sitting outside for the past half hour, staring at the wire tied around the banister, leading to the door handle. I think it'll hold. It should. It's got to be better than a bloody scarf.

I wonder if the sun's started to come up yet. It's got to be about time now.

I wish I knew what the time was. Can't find a single clock in the house. Not in this light. I almost feel like asking Edith what it says on her clock radio. I can't though. I promised her that I'd leave as soon as I secured the door. Last thing I want to do is worry her even more.

What the fuck am I gonna do about Sammy? I can't just sit and wait for him to show up. I have to think of a plan. Something that doesn't involve a horde of Necs eating me alive. Nothing I've done so far has brought me any closer to finding him. Not a single thing. And I can't exactly search every house on the street. Not with an army of Necs out there.

Maybe I should have just stayed behind the barricade. Waited for the Cleaners to do their Job. I would've been no closer to Sammy, but at least I'd be safe. At least I'd be around long enough to see him get out alive. Right now, for all I know, a pack of stinking Necs could be waiting outside, getting ready to storm the house.

Or maybe I should just hide 'til morning. Ride it out. Hopefully by then the government would have sent out some backup Cleaners.

Shit. What if the Necs have broken through the barricade? What if the whole of Bristol is infected? Maybe that's why it's taking them so long to get here. Perhaps it's *not* budget cuts. For all I know the entire city is overrun with Necs.

What the hell would we do then?

Stop it, Rob. You're being stupid. The rest of the world is exactly how it's always been: full of war, famine, and violence. Nothing's changed. And besides, Edith already said that the news is reporting usual stuff. No mention of an invasion.

Cover-up?

Shut up, Rob.

Suddenly I hear the noise of something falling and smashing inside Edith's room. I spring to my feet, clenching up.

I hear another noise. This time it's the sound of a cabinet or a chest of drawers crashing to the floor.

I double check the wire tied around the door handle. It seems safe enough. But I'm not exactly an expert on locking people in rooms.

Then the faint voice on the radio disappears with a loud shattering sound of plastic against the wall.

I can feel my heart racing once again as I fix my eyes on the door handle. I almost want to turn the knob to make sure it's locked from the inside. I know it is. I heard her do it. But I still have to fight the urge.

And then there's silence.

Dead silence. No radio. No footsteps. Nothing.

All I can hear is my heart pounding against my chest.

Leaning forward, I slowly place an ear to the

door to listen.

Still silence.

"Edith?" I whisper.

The sound of fists beating against the door causes me to move away in fright. I can hear her snarls as I back away towards the banister. The door vibrates as she kicks and punches at it; dust dropping from the top of the doorframe. I clench my fists tightly, bracing for her to break through the wood and come at me. The wire is holding—but for how long?

Shit! What the fuck do I do? Why did I have to say her name? Why couldn't I have kept my mouth shut? She might have turned and just stayed in the room. Peaceful.

I should never have come here in the first place. It was stupid. Should have stayed in my living room. Drinking beer. Should have never answered that *bloody* phone. At least Peter would have stayed put. He wasn't going anywhere until I showed up.

Time to go.

There's nothing more I can do for her. She's dead. The last thing she'd want me to do is stay and risk an attack from her.

And as I see a large split form at the centre of the door, I quickly make my way down the stairs.

Sorry, Edith.

I'm sorry I had to leave you.

I hope you find peace.

* * *

The garden is still dark, even though the sky is purple. Can't be much longer before the sun is up. Thank God. Although, it might make it a lot harder to get around in broad daylight.

I poke my head over Edith's wall and nervously peer into my garden. I can't see the Nec; the lighting is still too poor. Have to get the light-sensor back on. I wave my arm over the wall. Nothing happens.

Shit.

I listen carefully for any sounds. Can't seem to hear any movement.

Maybe it's died.

Outside Edith's backdoor is a bag of rubbish. I pick it up, and then launch it over the wall. The light comes on, instantly lifting the darkness from the garden.

The Nec has gone.

A shudder of panic washes over me, and I'm suddenly conscious of my surroundings, turning my head back and forth, scanning for the dead woman.

And then I notice something at the bottom of my garden. The Nec has somehow managed to drag herself blindly along, leaving behind a thick trail of blood. At first I wince at the sight. But then I almost feel pity—pity for an innocent woman whose body is being subjected to such hideous abuse. A woman who most likely started her day fairly normally, and then ended up been stripped of her skin. Stripped of her life, her family.

Of *everything* she held dear.

Fucking disease.

And what's driving the body? It's certainly isn't sight. She's got nothing left of her face. Can't be that. So what the fuck is it? The experts don't seem to know anything. It's all theories and bullshit. No real evidence. They say it's just muscle memory causing the limbs to move after the brain is dead.

They say the virus attacks the entire body. Not just the brain. Every cell in the body is infected with Necro-Morbus—with or without a head.

How screwed up is that!

I scale the wall and drop down into my garden, still with an eye firmly on the Nec. Doubt if she can still hear me. Can't be too careful, though. I've been wrong before. I rush into the house through the backdoor, locking it behind me.

The house is eerily quiet. It's still dark, but definitely lighter than it was a few hours ago. I walk down the empty hallway towards the living room. In the corner of my eye, I can just about make out a few photos on the wall beside me. Photos of Sammy. And Anna. *Thank God it's still dark.* Don't want to look at them. Not yet anyway.

It hurts too much.

Don't think I...

I enter the living room and go to the window. Pushing the curtain slightly to the side, I see out into the street. Everything seems quiet. Can't see any Necs from here.

Maybe it's over.

I go to the other end of the window for a better look. Still clear. A sudden feeling of relief washes over me as I press my face against the window to gain a further perspective.

"*Fuck!*" I mutter in fright as the putrid Nec passes the window. I swiftly release the curtain and drop down onto the floor.

Its shadow looms over me as I sit up against the wall. My muscles clench to bursting point; sweat building up on my brow. Please God, keep walking. Don't let them in here. Not now. Not in this house.

Give me that at least.

As the shadow finally disappears, I feel my body start to loosen up, and I let out a drawn out sigh of relief.

"Thank God."

After about a minute, I get up and sit on the single sofa-chair. Don't fancy sitting on the couch. Not with my back facing the window.

Sitting back—*exhausted*—my eyes stray to the TV. I fight hard not to switch it on. Would love to see the news now. Maybe Crandale will get a mention. Or at least the fuck up. Maybe they won't specify the area. Surely they'll have to eventually. *Shit*, I haven't heard a single helicopter since I got here. Not even a police siren for that matter. It's like the world outside no longer exists. Or more likely, Crandale no longer exists.

Should I watch the TV in the spare room? Don't think they'd see the light from up there.

No, I can't. The room will still glow too much, and then I'll have a hundred Necs at the door.

Not worth the risk. Wait 'til morning.

A few minutes go by, and I notice that the room is getting lighter. Either that, or my eyes are getting used to the darkness.

But the brighter it gets, the easier it is to see Sammy's baby photos on the wall. I fight the urge. With everything I've got. But the impulse overpowers me as my wandering eyes keep catching them.

Have to resist. Can't break down. Anna may be gone, but Sammy isn't. He's out there somewhere, and crying over some photo is hardly productive.

Have to stay strong. Can't let them break me. Not tonight.

As I listen to the clock ticking on the mantelpiece, thoughts of Edith fill my head. I see her sweet, innocent face; a woman who had no place in such a nightmarish situation. She should have lived out her life without having to deal with this *disease*.

But it found her in the end. It's only a matter of time before it finds us all. It took Anna, and now it's trying to take Sammy.

But I won't let it!

I hit the arm of the chair in anger as I stand up. "Fucking Necs!" I clench my fists tightly, and then drive one into the living-room door. The noise echoes around the room. I don't feel the pain in my knuckles. All I feel is a searing pain of frustration. Frustration because I can't find a way out of this Hell!

I pace the room, rambling incoherent thoughts; things I might do to anyone who lays a finger on my boy; things I might say to anyone who tries to stop me. No government official. No useless Cleaners. *No fucker's going to stop me!*

I can feel the rage as it boils the blood in my

body. I can't breathe. I need to do something. Need to act now. Can't stay here. Can't stay here waiting for help. Have to get out and find him.

"Fuck!" I scream as I punch the door again.

This time I feel the pain in my hand, but I ignore it. Instead, I storm out of the living room and march up to the front door, and then reach for the handle. "I've had enough of this shit! You fuckers can deal with *me!*"

My body is quivering with blind fury as I start to turn the handle.

"I'll kill every last one of you! Dead or not!"

I pull the door open a few inches.

"I'll tear your fucking heads off with my bare hands! I'll push your fucking eyeballs into your rotten skulls! There's nothing I—"

The faint morning light seeps through the quarter-open door, and I rapidly snap out of my furious rant. My stomach curdles at the thought of bursting out into the street and facing a crowd of Necs. Not just from the excruciating, horrifying agony of being eaten alive, but the thought of being unable to find Sammy.

I close the door quickly, and then silently and cautiously click the lock into place.

Dropping to the floor, I prop myself up against the door. I gaze at the dimly lit hallway and staircase as the sun slowly enters the house. I watch as the colour changes all around me. How it climbs the stairs, and brings the photos to life, one by one, painting the hallway. I see the picture of Sammy and Anna at the beach. And the one from last winter when it snowed. I can just about make out the furthest one. It's a wedding picture. Both of us stood on a bandstand. The happiest day of our lives. I can feel my heart ready to give in to sadness. But I can't look away. They have a hold over me. I can't resist. I'm not strong enough. I get up off the floor and walk up to the first photo. The one with Sammy and Anna at the beach. I pull it down from the wall and carry it back to the door. I drop down again, back against the door. My eyes are a blur with tears. They drip down onto the glass frame. I wipe them away from my eyes, and then from the photo. I can barely breathe. The anguish is too much. But I can't look away. Not anymore, as the grief overwhelms me.

This is my family.

There's no avoiding the pain. It'll be with me forever.

I need it. It's what'll drive me to find him.

And I *will* find him.

No matter how long it takes…

19

My eyelids slowly part. I can feel the bright morning light working its way into my eyes; blinding me. It's too much to bear so I close them again and try to sleep a little longer.

Suddenly my eyes burst open in fright, realising that I've fallen asleep.

Paranoia consumes me as I spring up onto my feet. Have the dead managed to get in while I was sleeping? Have I been bitten during the night?

I frantically pat myself down, looking for any obvious tears in my clothes, and blood stains.

I can't find any.

Thank God!

I try the front-door handle. Still locked. I creep into the living room; for all I know, an army of Necs could've smashed the window while I was sleeping. Stormed the house.

And leave me sleeping on the floor?

Not bloody likely.

Calm down, now. You're being ridiculous.

What if they thought I was dead? Left me alone?

Then they would have still tried to eat me. Necs are not exactly thoughtful creatures. They're not gonna just leave a perfectly good meal and look for the next.

It's just paranoia. Nothing else.

Nevertheless, I make my way through the kitchen, into the utility room, to make sure the backdoor is still locked.

It is.

Sighing loudly in relief, I leave the utility room, and then sit on a dining chair. Scanning the kitchen, I notice how different everything seems in the light of day; like waking from a nightmare. The gleam off the chrome microwave never looked so bright and polished. The hidden crumbs across the black kitchen worktop somehow more obvious. And the dusty footprints on the grey floor tiles, almost glowing in the morning light. I try to make out Anna's footprints, or Sammy's tiny ones—but all I see are my size tens, overlapping each other neatly like a necklace. As I hear the buzzing sound of the freezer, and the humming of the central heating, I know, without a shadow of a doubt, that I'm awake.

And morning is finally here.

But the nightmare is far from over. Hordes of Necs are most likely still clustered across Crandale. And Sammy's still out there. Somewhere.

I can feel the frustration build again. The same, consuming feeling that caused me to punch the door. I glance at my scuffed, bruised knuckles. I open and close my hand; clutching up in pain as I do.

I ain't punching any more walls. Not today. The only punching I'm gonna be doing is through the brain of some *bastard Nec!*

Plan.

I need a plan. Something solid.

Can't exactly burst out the front door and go on a killing spree. It's not a bloody film. I'd get overpowered in seconds. Have to think of a better plan of action. Could go out the back; try my luck through the back lanes. But then I risk getting blocked in. But then I'm blocked in if I opt to go out the front. Although at least out the front I'd have space to run 'round any Necs; even use the cars for cover. The back lanes, the only escape would be to climb onto one of the walls, and then drop down into a garden. That's if I *could* climb a wall. Some of those walls are high. Maybe eight or nine feet. I might be able to. If I had a run up.

I feel as if my body is in a vice, tightening with every second that passes. I try to shake it off but can't. Every possible action involves me, most likely, getting eaten alive, and no closer to Sammy. Because even if I *did* manage to go on a killing spree with a Samurai sword, taking off the heads of a hundred Necs—what good would it do? I have absolutely no clue where he is. For all I know, he's not even *in* Crandale. Just because he wasn't on the list. Maybe the list was wrong. If the Cleaners can't even sort out this place, then maybe they got the names mixed up. Disease Control might have him.

I stamp my fist hard on the table. "*Shit!*"

Staring down at the table, I notice a small, hardened stain on one of the tablemats. From its position, I assume that it's from Sammy. It's orange in colour, most likely from one of his yogurts. I smile at first, but then I feel a lump in my throat. I try to swallow it, but it's too jagged.

"Where are you, Sammy?" I mutter. "*Please.* Someone help me."

I gawk at the stain for maybe five minutes. I can't seem to move. I'm waiting to spring into action, but for some reason I don't.

Why not?

What the hell's wrong with me?

Am I scared?

Of course I'm scared. There's a shitload of Necs outside. Who *wouldn't* be scared? But nothing scares me more than losing him. I'd face a lifetime of them if it meant him being safe. I'd walk through—

Shit! The church!

I should have checked the bloody church!

I feel sick to my stomach at the thought of going back there. I stamp my fist down again on the table. I picture all those Necs, muzzled up and ready to be shipped over to Romkirk. Yeah, they may be restrained, but it wasn't exactly a picnic in the graveyard either. And by now, the place could be swarming with them, especially with the doors left open.

What am I saying? He's not in the church. He

can't be. If he's in there, then he's one of them—and I refuse to believe it. He's in one of these houses. Somewhere close. I'm certain. Anna probably took him to one of them when she knew she was infected. Maybe next door. Or the family opposite. And she must have asked them to keep him safe. And then Anna was too ill to get home. She probably turned on the way. She probably wondered off up Marbleview, towards Richmond, and then got picked up by one of the Cleaners. And then shipped over to me. The Cleaners never made it down here. He's probably safe and sound, just a few metres from here.

I know it. I can feel it.

I need to get a message to the neighbours.

I turn my head towards the phone fixed to the wall by the door. I spring up from the chair and pick up the receiver. And then I put it straight back down when I realise that I don't know anyone's numbers.

I should have gone back to the car for my mobile.

Stupid!

"Phone numbers," I mumble, scann
kitchen for Anna's phone book. "Where th
hell does she keep it?"

Does she even *have* one anymore?

Does anyone?

I rummage through the kitchen and uti
drawers, but all I find are loose batteries
and lots of keys—keys that I have absolute
what they open. I slam the last drawer
temper. "Stupid house! Can't find *anyth*
place!"

Leaving the kitchen, I head towards
room. Just as I reach the door, I notice
on the floor next to the front door.
frame from last night. The one with
Sammy at the beach. I walk over to it an
The picture sets off the same feelings
that I had last night. I shake them off
photo back over to the wall. I hang i
hook, making sure it's straight, and
quickly into the living room, trying de
to fall back into a depression.

Inside, I make my way over to

hoping to see Anna's phone book sitting next to it. I don't. I move over to the large cabinet on the other side of the room. Practically pulling out the contents of each of the three drawers, I still find nothing.

Realising the odds of me locating one are next to nothing, I give in and sit on the couch. Deflated.

If she *has* the numbers, they must be on her mobile. They've got to be. Maybe her phone is still here. Need to ring it. I grab the phone, but then put it back down when I realise that I have no idea what her number is.

Sighing loudly, I rub my forehead with my fingertips.

Think.

I'll have to just look for it.

Inspecting the mantelpiece, the top of the cabinet, and the couch, I find nothing. I exit the living room, hoping to have better luck searching the rest of the house. In the cupboard under the stairs, I check seven of Anna's handbags, and all six of her coat pockets—and still I come up empty.

I head upstairs, into the bathroom, and check the cupboard and the pockets of the dressing gown

hanging at the back of the door. Moving into Sammy's room, I check the bed, the cupboards, and the three shelves. And then I make my way into the last remaining room: our bedroom.

Knowing full well that this is my last hope of finding it, I practically ransack the room, like a cop on a drug raid. After several minutes of sieving through our belongings, emptying pockets onto the bed, and pulling out every box in the wardrobe, I give in and sit on the edge of the bed.

It's not here. She must have had it on her when she left. It's probably still over in Romkirk, melted to nothing in the furnace.

No, it's not. I bet she gave it to Sammy. Or whoever has him.

Shit! Why don't I know my own wife's phone number? What the hell's *wrong* with me? I'm a useless husband!

I bet she knew mine off by heart.

I'll have to check the neighbours' houses one by one. And then I'll have to cross over the road too.

It's not like I have much of a choice.

I walk over to the window. Standing to the side

of the open curtain, I look down into the street. Just opposite, maybe a few doors up, I see that Necs have forced their way into some poor bastard's house. The front door is just about on its hinges, and the glass of the front window is completely missing. I just hope to God that no one was home.

A sudden feeling of paranoia hits me. What if they force their way into here? What's to stop them? Should I have barricaded the windows and front door with planks of wood, like in the movies?

No. That's ridiculous. Where the hell would I find all that wood? And nails? Don't think I even have a *single* nail, let alone a boxful.

Or a hammer.

I look a little further up the street. I see a few more lurking along the pavements. Don't think I'd get all that far if I went out the front. I'd be swamped in seconds. I'll have to use the garden walls. At least I'm only likely to have to take out one or two at the most.

Only one or two?

I move to the other side of the window and look down the street. Five Necs are scattered about, shuffling aimlessly along the road and pavement, just waiting for some idiot to show his face. One of the Necs, a man, stops by the front door of a house. Something has caught his eye. He looks up at an open window above. I can hear the sound of his deathly cries from here.

The Nec suddenly drops to his knees.

And then onto his back.

"What the hell was that?" I mutter, pushing my face closer to the glass.

A second Nec, this time a woman, runs over to the motionless Nec. She's also looking up at the open window.

The woman collapses, smashing her face into the edge of the pavement.

"What the hell is going on?"

Focusing on the open window, I manage to catch a glimpse of a tall figure, wearing a white dressing gown.

It's a woman.

Janet Webber.

And she has a tranquiliser gun.

20

I grab the largest kitchen knife, and then bring it over to the front door, bracing before opening it. As soon as I do, I can hear the piercing screams of Necs close by. My hand is trembling as I open it a little more.

What the hell are you doing, Rob? You're an idiot. There's a good chance she hasn't even *seen* Sammy. What if you get yourself killed on the way over? How exactly is *that* gonna help him? Is it worth the risk?

Damn right it is!

What choice do I have? I'm gonna lose my mind if I stay in here a minute longer. Doing *nothing*. Plus, she has a tranq gun.

All I've got is a blunt bread knife.

I have to get to her.

I take in a couple of deep breaths, and then step out onto the pavement. The cold winter air hits me in the face. It feels good, almost blocking out the gut-wrenching fear that's pulsating through my body. With the knife pointed outwards, I carefully close the front door, and then creep along the wall. I reach Anna's car and crouch down, viewing Janet Webber's house through the car windows. I see two Necs wandering along the pavement about a hundred metres down, and another two just sitting against one of the houses, as if conserving energy.

How the fuck am I supposed to do this? If the Necs don't spot me, there's a bloody good chance Janet will shoot me. How is she supposed to know that I'm not one of them? If I shout up to her, tell her who I am, then I'm *bound* to draw attention. And if the Necs don't eat me, then I'm just gonna lead them straight into her house.

Nothing's bloody easy.

I scan the street up and down, hoping to see something to spark off an epiphany, the perfect strategy. But all I see are more Necs, maybe ten or twelve limping around the cars, as if patrolling Marbleview.

I'm fucked.

Totally *fucked!*

Think, Rob. How did you get Mark Turner's attention when he was grounded for two weeks?

Long before mobile phones were around?

Stones!

You threw a stone at his window!

Looking down at the curb, I see a few small stones. I gather them up and slither towards the next car. Then the next, until I'm opposite to Janet's house. Way too close to a couple of Necs though. If I could throw a little better, then maybe I wouldn't have to be so near. All those years of knowing that my throwing skills were shit, and telling myself that it didn't matter—well fuck me, it matters today.

I launch the first stone up at the top window. It misses, hitting the windowsill, and then it drops down onto the road. I freeze as I wait for the stone to grab a Nec's attention.

It doesn't. Thank God.

I sigh in relief. Taking another stone from my hand, I straighten a little, hoping to get a better shot a second time. I throw the stone as if my life depended on it.

It hits the window, bounces off, and then lands on a car bonnet. The noise of metal manages to alert a wandering Nec. I drop to the floor, rolling nearly underneath the car to hide. I can hear its footsteps scrape lazily against the concrete from across the road. Then the sound changes. I can now hear the sound of hard tar rubbing against its shoe as it crosses towards me.

The sound is getting closer.

And closer.

It finally stops at the other side of the car. Gingerly, I roll even further under the car until I'm staring up at a rusty exhaust pipe. I imagine terrible images of a rotting Nec crouching down to peer under, and then crawling towards me; its teeth snarling; mouth foaming with rage.

But it doesn't.

Instead, the Nec just carries on stumbling down the street in the direction of Rose Avenue. Closing my eyes, I sigh as relief washes over me. I wait about a minute and then roll back out onto the pavement. I pinch a third stone and draw my arm back. I try to steady my breathing as I aim it at the window. Releasing the stone, it catapults across the road and hits, smack-bang, in the centre of the window. I silently celebrate by clenching a fist tightly. Finally, a little luck!

Suddenly a figure comes to the window. It's Janet Webber. I'm shaking with excitement and panic. Panic at the thought that she won't see me, or even let me through the door. For all she knows I could be infected. I stand up and foolishly wave the knife up to her. She sees me immediately.

Unfortunately, she's not the only one.

Turning my head, I see four Necs running at me; screaming with feral rage. My eyes broaden in horror. *What the fuck have I done? How could I have been so stupid?* Their screams alert two more. I start to run down Marbleview. But before I get even fifty-metres, I run into another three Necs bursting out from a house. Sprinting around them, I slam my chest into a parked car. I fall down to the pavement, onto my back, losing the knife in the process. I can't breathe; the wind knocked out of me. The two decrepit Necs are on top of me, their jaws snapping at my skin. I kick hysterically, twisting my body around as they try to move past my legs. Even through the snarls and desperate moans, I can hear the sound of heavy footsteps coming towards me.

It's only a matter of time before I'm finished. I manage to grab the wrists of one Nec and push him clear of me. Another bites down hard. I can feel its jaws lock down around my leg like a pit-bull. I convulse hard as if in the middle of an epileptic fit, and the Nec lets go of my leg. I kick out as hard as I can and catch it square in the jaw. I hear the bone shatter. The morning sunlight is fading. The sheer volume of bodies has blocked it out. I'm surrounded. No matter how hard I fight, there's just too many of them. With every ounce of strength left in me, I try to stand. But the weight is too much.

This is it.

I've never been so terrified; so unprepared for death.

Not now.

Not like this.

Not when I've—

I hear a faint thud. Then another. And another...

The sunlight begins to seep through again. Suddenly I'm locked in battle with just two. Exhausted beyond comprehension, I struggle to free myself from their stronghold. The stench of rotten bodies pulls me back from the darkness. I'm still alive. And I hear a voice. It's a woman's voice.

"Get up!" she cries. "Come on! Get up! Now! Move!"

Without even realising, the two Necs are no longer moving. I push their heavy, dead bodies from me, and scramble to my feet. I see Janet Webber, wearing a white dressing gown, driving her foot down into the face of a Nec. She has a gun in her right hand. Disorientated, I'm unable to find the words to express how grateful I am. So relieved. As if I'd died and been pulled back down to earth by a giant white angel.

"Follow me, Rob," she says, pulling out a blood-soaked slipper from the Nec's face, and then motioning with her head for me to go with her. She then runs off to her house. I follow closely behind, still struggling to comprehend what just happened.

Inside the house, Janet slams the front door shut and slides a large bolt-lock across. She even puts on the chain. Groaning loudly, clearly drained, she runs her fingers through her long, wavy ginger hair.

I slide down the wall, into a sitting position on the cold tiled floor. I sigh loudly, still worn-out from the attack. I can feel my body slowly begin to loosen up. I look down at my hands; they're shaking uncontrollably. I breathe slowly to settle them. But just as feel them steady, I suddenly remember about the Nec that bit down on my leg. The Nec's spit-covered bite mark is still visible on my trousers. I straighten out the crease mark as I inspect for blood and holes.

There are none.

Unconvinced, I leap to my feet and unclip my belt buckle, and then pull down my trousers. After thoroughly examining both legs, unbelievably I can't find a single mark. I shake my head in astonishment.

Thank God for thick trousers.

"You're lucky," Janet says, her lofty body propped up against the wall, towering me without effort. "I thought they'd bitten you. It's a miracle they didn't tear you to *pieces*."

The horrid memory of being pinned to the ground sends a cold shudder through my body. I try to shake it off as I pull up my trousers. "Tell me about it. I can't thank you enough, Janet. I thought I was done for. I thought…"

"Well, you're safe now, Rob. They ain't coming through *that* bloody door. Not if I've got any breath left in me."

I nod, even though the last thing I feel is safe. Saf*er* maybe. But definitely not safe. "Thank God for that gun," I say; attention still very much on the front door, and whether that lock and chain is enough to keep them out.

"Yeah—don't I know it," she replies, slipping the tranq gun into her deep, dressing-grown pocket. She pulls out a packet of cigarettes and a blue lighter from the other pocket. She slides one out, puts it into her mouth, and lights it. Tucking her fringe behind her ear, she takes in a long, deep drag as if to calm herself, and then blows out a huge puff of smoke. "You want one?" she asks me, pointing the packet at me.

I shake my head. "No. No thanks. I don't smoke. Well, not since college."

"I think today's a good a day as any to start again." Motioning with her head, she points the pack at me again. "Go on. You could you use one. It'll calm your nerves a little. One won't kill you."

Looking down at my leg again, a quiver of 'what-if' pulsates through my body. The thought of getting infected. Turning into one of those animals.

One cigarette is the least of my worries.

I nod, and then slide one out from the pack. Janet leans forward to light it. Taking in the nicotine, tasting the tobacco, a sudden rush of nostalgia hits me; it takes me away from the death all around me; away from my desperate hunt for Sammy. It nearly takes away the memory of Anna and what I had to do.

But only for a second.

I take another drag, hoping that the effect is repeated. But nothing happens. Just that foul taste of tobacco that I trained myself to hate. The stink that repelled Anna whenever I snuck a quick cigarette after a few drinks. Nothing more than that.

I cough loudly as I hand the cigarette back over to her, shaking my head, struggling to catch my breath. Janet smiles tightly as she takes it from me.

God, I wish she had some weed instead.

"So what's the story?" Janet asks. "How did you find me? I didn't think there was anyone still alive out there. Seems like the whole of Crandale's turned."

"I know. It's bad. The entire area is cordoned off by police. And Necs have pretty much wiped out all the Cleaners. I spoke to one yesterday. He told me that there was just too many them. I guess any still alive have left already. Who knows."

"So how are you here? Where've you been hiding?"

"Home. Just up there," I gesture with my head over to my house. "I've been there since yesterday. I've been there since, well…Anna died. So—"

"Your wife? Oh, Jesus Christ. I'm so sorry, Rob."

"She got infected the day before yesterday. And then I found out in work, so I managed to sneak past the barricade and in through the church. *That* wasn't easy, I can tell you—especially since the place was swarming with Necs. I mean literally crawling wall to wall. And the rest of Crandale is pretty much infested with them too. Up and down the streets.

They're everywhere. Doorways. Houses. It's no wonder the Cleaners lost control. They're gonna need a small *army* to clear this place. Seriously. It's really bad."

"I know. I shot down a few earlier."

"Yeah, I saw you from the window. That's why I came here. You're the first person I've seen in a while. And you're definitely the first person I've seen with a tranquiliser gun."

She pulls the gun back out from her pocket.

"How did you get hold of it?" I ask.

"I found it yesterday. One of those Cleaners got attacked just outside the front door there. They tore him to shreds. Before he turned, his belt broke off. I waited 'til he wandered off somewhere and then snuck out and grabbed it. It had his tranquiliser gun, and an almost-full magazine clipped to the top. So every time a few congregate outside, I use it. Just to keep them out, ya know. But the effects don't last that long. Sometimes just minutes. There's no telling."

"Yeah, I know. They're only really meant to bring them down so they can be bagged up and shipped to the furnace."

"Oh, right. How do you know so much?"

I contemplate telling her that I saw it online or on a documentary, but instead I decide to tell her the truth. The woman just saved my life. "I work for a company called Romkirk Limited. It's a place where Necs are shipped. They call us *Burners*—and it's our job to incinerate the infected in the furnace."

"*Oh God*. I had no idea. I thought you worked in some office or something."

"No. Sometimes I wish I did."

"So you *burn* them?"

I nod.

"So do they ever try to cure them?" she asks. "I mean, before you dispose of them?"

"No. There is no cure, Janet. How *could* there be? They're dead. Their bodies are just walking disease. Nothing else."

"Oh, right. See I've always found that hard to swallow. How can something that's dead still be able to walk? *And* run. Those ones that attacked you looked pretty quick on their feet. Even quicker than *me*."

I shrug. "Scientists are always changing their minds on the whole Necro-Morbus thing. Some say it's just motor-functions powered by adrenalin. And others say it's the virus taking over the entire corpse. The truth is: no one really knows for sure. Not yet anyway."

"I read in the paper last year that they're not dead. It's just an advanced form of necrosis. And that the person is very much alive inside, but just trapped in some deep coma."

"Don't believe everything you read. There's always some stupid story in the paper telling us that broccoli is good for you one minute, and then the next it's giving you cancer. No, Janet, trust me when I say this: they're dead. There is no cure."

"How can you be so sure?"

"Because of my job. It's hard doing what I do and not take an interest in it. It's one of the reasons I applied. I've always been fascinated by the disease. Ever since the first case."

"So what if you're wrong?"

I run my hand through my sweat-soaked hair and look her square in the eye. "Yesterday...I had to burn my wife in the furnace."

Janet's eyes widen in shock. I can see her jaw literally drop. And who could blame her? Maybe I shouldn't have told her. Or least avoided telling her so dramatically.

But I did. And I can't take it back now.

"I'm so sorry, Rob. I had no idea. It must have been—"

I nod, knowing exactly what she was about to say. "Worst day of my life. Bar none. And the thought of losing my son as well is just too much. So I desperately need your help, Janet. My little boy is somewhere in Crandale. Anna was probably the last person he was with. He's four years old. Blond hair. I don't know what he'd be wearing. The last thing he had on was his pyjamas. Maybe he's still in them. I don't know. They were light blue. The ordinary type with the buttons down the front. Have you seen him? Or at least heard something? I don't know what else to do. *Please.*"

"What's your little boy called?" Janet asks.

"It's Sammy. Sammy Stephenson."

"Well, Rob—you're in luck," she says with a

smile. "He's here."

My ears almost don't register her words; the words I've been longing for since I crossed the barricade. Did I imagine them? Am I still disorientated and delirious from the attack?

"Say that again?" I ask her; leaning my head in closer as if hard of hearing.

"I said he's here. Your son. Sammy? He's downstairs. In the basement. He's safe. He's with my husband and two children."

Suddenly I'm lightheaded with joy and disbelief. My stomach feels just about ready to puke up all over the floor. Don't know why. The last thing I thought I'd be feeling is sick. Crying? Yes. Sick to the stomach? Definitely not. But here I am standing in Janet Webber's front hall, listening to the news I would have gladly tolerated a lifetime of hell to hear. Suddenly the world outside is a minor inconvenience. A bad day at the office. A shitty holiday. Nothing like the sick and twisted world I've had to endure.

Janet Webber: my new favourite neighbour. Never again will I refer to her as a weirdo.

"Is he all right?" I ask; voice shaky. "Is he infected?"

Janet smiles, shaking her head. "No, he's fine, Rob. Not a scratch on him. He's been down the basement since yesterday. That's where we've been hiding since this whole mess started. Safest place in the house." She points to a door just past the staircase. "The basement is through there."

Heading towards the door, I quietly thank her. When I reach the door, I turn the handle and open it. I see the wooden stairs through the dimly-lit bulb, just above them. The moment I place my foot down on the first step, I hear a faint thud. And a sharp pain at the back of my left shoulder. Bemused, I turn and see Janet standing behind me, with the gun pointed at me. I see her mouth the words, 'I'm sorry', as I plummet down the rickety staircase.

I don't feel the pain as my head slams into the wall, and then onto the middle step, until finally onto the hard basement floor.

As I lie on my side, unable to move even a finger, I hear the echoed footsteps of Janet Webber coming down the stairs.

I see her royal-blue slippers just inches from my face.

The colours all around me are bleeding into one.

All I see are swirling colours. A vortex of light and colours.

Am I dead?

Am I one of them?

Is this what it feels like to be...

21

I can hear the rumbling sound of the furnace as it fires up. I feel the heat on my skin. For some reason, it feels good. Good to be back at work. Back to earning some cash. Vegas is just around the corner. Can't set foot in those casinos without a decent amount of money to blow. It wouldn't be right. But the greatest thing about being in Romkirk again is the routine, the normalcy of it all. Although, to most people, normalcy might be some way off from burning reanimated corpses in a furnace—especially for a living.

Not me, though.

This is where I belong, where I was always going to end up. A career.

It's not exactly glamorous, or dignified, but neither is cutting someone up with a scalpel then sticking them back together, or shooting someone down in some shithole country in the middle of nowhere.

Yeah, this is where I belong.

This is me.

Wheeling the stretcher over to the furnace, I can't help but notice how still the body bag seems. Not even a flicker. Even the most heavily sedated Necs twitch after this long in transit. I'm a slave to curiosity once again as I slowly unzip the yellow bag. I open it about halfway down, and then grab each end of the opening, and spread them apart. Just to see. See for myself who the poor bastard is this time. See which innocent bystander has been taken by this putrid, soul-sucking disease.

I drop to my knees in anguish, almost choking on my own turmoil.

Sammy.

Is this some kind of a prank? A sick joke?

Is this really my *son*, stuffed into a body bag, seconds from being burned?

I get back up onto my feet, holding onto the sides of the stretcher to stop my legs from buckling. I take another look down. It *is* him. It *is* my son. My precious, innocent little boy, lying down; his skin pale and lifeless like a China doll.

I won't burn him in the furnace. Not now. Not ever. I'd rather *die* than let him burn.

Suddenly his eyes open and he springs upright, screaming as if waking from a nightmare.

From fright, I stumble backwards, crashing into another stretcher. I fall to the floor, my back pressed up against one of its metal legs. I watch in horror as Sammy starts to slither out of the body bag like a snake, his jaw snapping and snarling at me.

"Sammy, it's me," I say, "It's Daddy. There's nothing to worry about. No one's gonna harm you. *Please.* Don't you recognise me? It's *Daddy.*"

A shadow slowly looms over me from behind, and then I feel something cold grab the back of my neck. I turn my head and look up. I see Anna; her decaying face peering down from the stretcher; her arm, grey with decomposition, reaching down at me. I scurry across the floor on my hands and knees, pushing myself up onto my feet, over to the open furnace. I can feel and hear the blistering heat burn the hairs on the back of my head. Both Anna and Sammy are now off the stretchers and are limping slowly towards me, their mouths dripping with saliva and rage. Edging ever closer to the fire behind me, I feel the flames biting at my exposed skin. Suddenly, Anna bolts at me, driving both her palms into my chest. I fly back into the heart of the furnace. I scream out to them to help me, but my words are melting by the inferno.

Along with my skin.

The last thing I see before my eyes burst is Sammy, as he pushes the large red button.

The giant flames have turned into flashes of light.

I can no longer hear the rumbling sound of the furnace. All I can hear are echoes of muffled voices. Like voices from a busy swimming pool. *Like the sounds of...*

Am I dead?

Am I one of them?

Is this what it feels like to be...

* * *

"Can you hear me?"

Who said that?

I try to focus but can't. All I can see are blurred images.

I see something move.

Is there someone there?

Please help me I—

"You need to open your eyes. My name is Sandra. Can you hear me?"

Is that a voice? Sandra?

Who the hell is Sandra?

"Wake up. Can you hear me? You need to wake up."

The silhouette of a person slowly forms. The flames are long gone.

It's a woman. It's...

"...Anna?"

"No, it's not Anna," I hear a female voice say. "It's Sandra. My name is Sandra Ross. I'm one of your neighbours."

My blurred vision starts to dwindle as my eyes begin to focus. I'm in a dark room, with a faint light coming from the top of a staircase to the right of me. Sitting to my left, her thin body leaning over to face me, is a woman. Mid-forties, maybe fifty, wearing trousers or jeans. And a thick, reddish jumper. Light-brown hair. Although it could be blonde. Too hard to make out in such poor lighting. "Where am I?" I ask the woman. But before she can even answer, I remember exactly where I am.

Janet Webber's basement.

"How's the head?" she softy asks me, her voice weak and croaky.

Suddenly recalling my plummet down the stairs, I start to feel a dull ache at the side of my head. I reach up to touch it only to find a sharp pain in my left shoulder, and my wrists tied together with thin rope. I tug on them hard and hear the sound of metal rasping. I see a thicker rope attached to my wrists leading to a large pipe behind me. I pull on it, but the pipe is fixed securely to the wall. I look down at my ankles; they're also bound together by rope.

"What the fuck is going on?" I snap, a jolt of panic hitting me as my clarity returns. I thrash desperately at my restraints, trying to pry my hands and legs free to no avail.

"That woman upstairs is Janet Webber." She points with her tied wrists to the ceiling. "She's been my neighbour for twenty years. The twisted bitch drugged you and brought you here."

"*Jesus Christ*," I say, tugging frantically at the rope, ignoring the ache in my shoulder. "How long have you been down here?"

"Almost two days. But it's hard to keep track."

"*Two days?*"

"We haven't eaten *or* drunk anything since we got here." She motions with her head to my right.

Turning my throbbing head, I see a mound of white beside me. Leaning in closer, I try to make out what it is.

It's a Cleaner. Male.

He's passed out in a slump; arms twitching slightly; his breathing erratic.

"*Oh my God*," I blurt out. "What the hell does she *want* with us?"

"It's probably best if I don't tell you."

"What's the hell is *that* supposed to mean?"

Sandra sighs, glimpses down to the side of her, and then whispers, "Because I don't want to scare him."

"Scare who?" I ask, impatiently.

"The little boy."

I shudder for a moment as I struggle to see past her.

Suddenly I'm no longer in a dusty, cluttered old basement, restrained by my wrists and feet, surrounded by a rank, musty smell.

Suddenly I'm *exactly* where I'm supposed to be.

"Sammy?" I delicately call out.

Please let it be him. Please let it be my little boy.

Please let it be—

"Daddy?" I hear a child whisper, his words groggy and broken.

Huddled up against Sandra, a small boy, four years old, wearing blue pyjamas, slowly pops his head up.

It's Sammy.

Is this a dream? Am I still passed out at the bottom of the stairs?

Is it really my son?

Please let it...

"Daddy?" I hear him say again.

I start to cry.

I can't help it. It feels like the same bout of tears from when he was born. An uncontrollable surge of bottled up emotions; all flooding out the very second I held him in my arms. "*You're really here,*" I tell him, my words drowning in tears. "Are you okay? Did she hurt you?"

He shakes his head, and then he starts to sob loudly. "Where've you been, Daddy? You were gone for so long. Where's Mammy?"

Sniffing loudly, I try to compose myself. "Don't cry, Sammy. I'm sorry. I've been looking everywhere for you. I couldn't find you. But I'm here now. You don't have to worry. Daddy's found you."

"I'm scared, Daddy. There's a nasty woman upstairs."

"Don't worry about her. She won't hurt you. I promise."

"It's all right, Sammy," Sandra says, pulling him close. "We're just playing a game. Remember? It's like hide and seek. And the lady upstairs is just pretending to be mean. That's all. Like a pantomime."

"Yeah, that's right," I say, trying to block out the panic. "Just a silly game. There's nothing to worry about."

"We've been playing other games too, haven't we, Sammy?" Sandra says, forcing a smile. "In case we got bored down here."

Sammy nods.

"Oh, that sounds like fun," I say, struggling to play along. "What games have you played?"

"'I spy'," he tells me, his tears subsiding.

"Oh, yeah. That's my *favourite* game."

Sammy huddles up even closer to Sandra; his affection for her obvious. "I like Auntie Sandra."

"We've been telling stories, too," Sandra continues. "Funny ones. Haven't we?"

He nods again, confusion and worry ingrained on his face.

"*Has* she," is all I can manage as another tear rolls down my cheek.

Sandra spots it. "He's all right, Rob," she says, trying to reassure me.

But nothing about this situation is all right.

Far from it.

"She's given him a little water to drink," she continues. "A few hours ago. And a little food. While you were unconscious. He's the only one

223

who's had anything." She shrugs her shoulders. "So that's something at least."

Sighing, I lean back against the wall. "Jesus Christ—what the *hell* does she want with us? I mean, what possible—"

Sandra puts her index finger over her mouth to shush me, and then points to the opposite wall. The area is even darker, almost impossible to see anything apart from the outlines of boxes and other piles of junk.

"What's there?" I whisper. "I can't see any—"

The entire room starts to vibrate as the sound of heavy footsteps fills the air. Sandra shuffles back against the wall like a frightened animal; pulling Sammy with her.

"You're *awake* then," Janet Webber casually says as she reaches the foot of the stairs. "About time, too. I was beginning to worry."

She walks over to the Cleaner and then prods him with her foot. Apart from a slight whimper, he doesn't respond. "How's he been?" she asks, kneeling down beside him.

"How'd you *think* he's been, Janet?" Sandra

snaps. "He's bloody dying! You need to get him to a hospital. Now this minute."

"And how am I supposed to do that? Fly him out? The whole of Crandale is blocked off. We could be trapped here for *weeks*. Maybe even *months*. And it's only a matter of time before they shut off the power. But us Webbers are always prepared. You won't see *us* getting left behind. *No* bloody way. We've got everything we need right here. Food. Water. Even Power." She glances over to a small generator. It's resting on top of a washing machine by the stairs. "What *else* do you need?"

"Don't be an idiot, Janet," Sandra continues. "They're not gonna cut off the power. Why the hell would they? It's only been a couple of days. You're talking as if it's the bloody apocalypse or something. The police are probably outside the blockade, getting ready to put an end to all this mess."

"And you're sure about that are you, Sandra?"

"Yes, I am. I'm bloody positive."

"Then why haven't we heard any police sirens— or helicopters? How come it took just a matter of hours to infect this place?"

"*I* don't bloody know. All I know is that you've kept us all locked up for the past two days, without food *or* water, and you've got a poor man lying on your basement floor, about to die! So tell me, Janet, how the *hell* is this gonna help your situation? Come on, Janet, because I'd *love* to know."

"There haven't been any helicopters or police sirens because the whole city's been infected."

"That's *bullshit!* And you know it!"

"No, it's not."

"Yes, it is. It takes time to decontaminate a place as big as this."

"What do you want with us?" I ask, as warily as I can.

Janet turns to me, and then looks over at Sammy; her eyes showing flickers of remorse at the sight of him. "The same reason *you* came here."

"What do you mean? I came here looking for my son."

"Yeah. Exactly. You came here looking to save your family. And that's why I've kept you here. *All* of you."

"Keep your voice down, Janet," Sandra warns

her. "Don't tell him in front of his boy. At least give him that."

"What are you talking about?" I ask. "What possible reason would you have to keep us down here? Especially with things the way they are. We should be *helping* each other."

Janet walks over to the opposite wall, into the darkness. "We *are* helping each other." I then hear the sound of a light flicking on. Suddenly I see Janet standing against the wall, next to three more people restrained by their wrists and feet. A bald man, late-forties, a redheaded boy in his late-teens, and a thin redheaded girl, no older than seven. The sight of them causes me to shuffle back and clench up in revulsion.

All three prisoners are dead.

"What the hell have you *done* to them?" I scream, scurrying backwards against the wall in fright. "*For Christ's sake!* How could you do—"

"I haven't *done* anything to them," Janet replies; her tone bitter, as if insulted by the very thought of mistreatment. "This is my *family*, Robert. This is why I brought you here."

"What the hell are you talking about? They're *dead!*"

"No, they're not dead," Janet replies. "They may *look* dead to someone like you—but they're very much alive." She peers down at them—beaming with pride—as if their bodies weren't perished and stinking of rot, as if they were nothing more than an ordinary family sat in front of the TV. "They just need a little help. That's all. They're just sick."

"Why the hell didn't you call someone? You could have helped them. You could have got an antiviral shot at the hospital."

Janet looks at me in disgust. "What, so someone like *you* can come along and burn them like vermin? Like you did you own *wife?* Like you did with your little boy's mother?"

I turn to Sammy in horror. He's still huddled up tight to Sandra, her arms covering his eyes. *Please, God don't let him understand what she said.*

Please...

"Look, Janet," I say, "whatever you think you can do to save them, just let us go. We've done nothing to you and your family. And I'm sorry for what's happened to them. I really am. I know what it's like to lose someone close. But keeping them here is only gonna make things worse. Much worse. They can still spread the disease. Even after they've died."

"They're not dead!" Janet screams, causing me to jolt back with fright.

Janet's husband slowly begins to stir. He seems far more decomposed than his children; eye sockets deeply sunken; his arms thin and wasted; lips and gums receding. He opens his mouth, and then suddenly the room comes alive with an ear-shattering growl.

Her two children have woken too, snarling and squirming, trying to free themselves from their tied limbs. Janet moves away from her husband as he tries to bite at her ankle.

"Look what you've done now, you idiot!" Janet snaps. "You've woken them up!"

"For God's sake," I plead, "You have to get out of this basement. *All* of us do. It's too dangerous. The longer you leave them tied down here, the more aggressive they're gonna get. Please, Janet—listen to me. I know what I'm talking about. They could escape. Infect us all. And what good would that do?"

"You don't have to be nervous 'round them. They won't escape. I've tied 'em down even tighter than you three. They ain't going anywhere—and neither are you."

"What the hell are you talking about? How is keeping us locked down here ever going to help you?"

"She's got a plan," Sandra says, sarcastically. "Haven't you, Janet? You've *found* the cure. Isn't that right?"

"What cure?" I ask. "There's no *cure*. They're dead. It's just the disease running through their bodies. There's nothing anyone can do."

"Oh, she's found a cure, all right," Sandra continues. "She thinks that giving her family *fresh meat* will somehow bring them back to life."

I gasp in horror, knowing exactly what Sandra means by *fresh meat*.

Suddenly I can feel my heart beating hard against my chest. I'm gasping for air. The room is spinning fast, out of control. I try to focus but can't. The light is getting brighter and brighter. Blinding me.

Need to get out of here.

Can't breathe.

I'm still dreaming.

That's all.

I'm still asleep...

But then my eyes start to focus again, and I see the cold, desperate look on Janet's face, and the pool of dried blood and torn flesh on the floor around her family.

And I can see all too clearly that I'm awake.

And this nightmare has only just begun.

22

Janet Webber.

At first, she just seemed little more than a middle-aged tomboy when I saw her shooting Necs from the window. But now, as I watch her hack off the limbs of the Cleaner with a meat cleaver, and pass them down to her rotten husband and two children, I now know different. I now know how twisted and deeply disturbed she is.

Was it the loss of her family that has sunk her to this level? Or has she always been so…lost?

Impossible to tell.

What I do know is that no matter what life throws at me, no matter how hard and unbearable it might be—I would *never* resort to cold-blooded murder!

Never!

"Can't let them have the entire body," Janet says, wiping the sweat from her brow. "Malcolm will hog all the meat. He's always been like that. Can't have my kids *starving* to death—not while I'm still their mother."

I can hear Sammy crying, his face buried deep into Sandra's shoulder. From the look on Sandra's face, it seems like she's holding back a flood of vomit. But who could blame her? Don't even know if it's the sight of the limbs being cut off and eaten—or the fact that one of us is next in line.

I try to look away from the putrid horror, but for some reason I can't pull my eyes away. I'm drawn to watch the vile acts of murder. Maybe I've just desensitised myself from working at Romkirk. Or maybe I just need to see what's to become of me, to see what I'm up against.

To see—

"You're a sick!" Sandra yells out; her words muffled with anguish and revulsion. "You're a murderer, Janet! A sick, depraved murderer!"

Janet doesn't even look up at her as she begins cutting down on the Cleaner's last remaining leg. "I'm a lot of things, Sandra—but a murderer is not one of them."

"Then what the hell would you call it?"

"Survival."

"How the *hell* is killing an innocent man, *survival?*

233

He's done *nothing* to you. Absolutely *nothing* at all. He came here to keep us all safe. And you've just killed him in cold blood."

"If this is what it takes to cure my family, then one bloody Cleaner is worth it."

"You're a psycho! There is no cure! Your family is *dead!* When are you going to get it through your *thick skull?*"

Janet's chopping suddenly becomes a lot more vicious, clearly angered by Sandra's comments. I look over at Sammy; he's still huddled up close to Sandra.

Thank God he hasn't been alone down here. Thank God for Sandra.

"Look, Janet," I say, "I know you're hurting. But feeding them won't bring them back. Please, just take a moment and step back—then you'll see how *crazy* all this is."

Janet stops cutting, and lets go of the meat cleaver. She sits, just a metre from her daughter, next to the washing machine, and then looks over to me. "I'm well aware how ridiculous this may seem. I really do. But I have to. I know they may look dead, and I know that the books and the TV say that they are. But I know, with every ounce of my heart, that my family is still alive. Yeah, they may be lost for the moment, trapped in a deep, dark coma, inside their decaying bodies," she shakes her head in denial, "but I don't believe that God would ever allow the dead to just walk around like this."

"We don't think you're crazy because you believe your family is alive," Sandra interrupts. "It's the fact that you just *butchered* that poor man to death."

"Why don't you shut your *fucking mouth*, Sandra. They need to feed. They need human meat. *Fresh* meat. It's the only thing they *can* eat. Do you really think that this was my first plan of action? Do you really think this was an easy decision for me? Well, it wasn't. *That* you can be sure of. I tried everything. When Malcolm first turned, I gave him raw, animal meat—he didn't touch it. Christ, the only thing that came close was dog meat. Our three dogs were the first to go, followed by any dog I could get hold of around Crandale. But it just wasn't good enough. Only when he ate Paul Henry from next door, did he start to settle, as if satisfied. And Paul was just an accident. I never wanted him to die. I loved him. He was like family to us. He was one of Malcolm's best friends. But once he got hold of him, he wouldn't stop tearing him to pieces. It was horrible!"

Janet shakes her head in disgust. "But that's when I realised that he needed live, human meat to survive. So I just had to take Paul's wife, Alison— for Sophie and Jack." She glimpses down at the dried blood on the floor by her family. "I just had to. I had no choice. This *is* the cure. The *only* cure. This course of action *will* bring them back—I just know it. Sophie's already started showing signs of calm. She hasn't tried to bite me since yesterday. And I'm sure her skin is getting better too. It's looking a lot clearer."

I listen to Janet as she gives her reasons for such a despicable act, and I can't help but feel sorry for her. Maybe she *was* driven to this only by the loss of her family. Maybe it wasn't something that's always been inside her—brewing slowly—waiting to come to the surface.

Nevertheless, she's a sick, vile murderer. Even if

she *could* plead temporary insanity in a court of law—that won't stop me from killing her *and* her family to get us the fuck out of here!

Have to be smart about this. Screaming at her is only gonna make matters worse. Have to keep her cool; keep her talking.

For Sammy.

"Janet, I understand," I say, softly. "I know what it feels like to want to keep your family safe. I knew that whatever was in Crandale didn't matter to me. Nothing inside could compare to the thought of losing Sammy. *Nothing*. No disease. No Necs. Just the love for my little boy. See, Janet, you and I are the same. We're prepared to do *anything* to save our family. So please, at least let my son go. He's already lost his mother to this disease. Don't make him go through anything else. I'll gladly take his place. I won't put up a fight. I promise. Just let him go. He's got his grandmother to look after him. He'll be all right. *Please*, Janet, I'm begging you. You know it's the right thing to do."

The room falls silent. All I can hear is the sound of her family chewing on lumps of flesh. I try to block out the gut-wrenching noise and focus on Janet. I have to get through to her. I can do this. I know I can. If I can burn Necs for a living, then I'm sure I can get through this. She's just a woman who's lost her family. If I can sympathise, try to think on her level, then maybe I stand a chance. A slim one.

It's not like I have any other options.

"I couldn't let him go even if I wanted to," Janet says, picking up the meat cleaver again, continuing to chop down on the leg. "There'd be no point."

"Why? Surely you can think about it. He's just a little boy. *Please, Janet.*"

"There'd be no point—he wouldn't last thirty-seconds outside. Not with all those Necs running about. There's a hundred of 'em. Maybe more. At least down here he can spend his last few hours with his father."

I feel an uncontrollable tightening of my entire body, consuming me. Frustration and anger are strangling me. I try anxiously to hold back my emotions, but it's impossible. "Please, Janet, I'm begging you. Let's all go then. We can keep him safe. Please. You don't have to do this. I'm begging you."

But my words of desperation go unheard as she tears off the leg from the Cleaner's hip joint. It gives off a horrid popping sound. I hear Sandra throw up over herself as Janet passes the leg over to her husband. The three Necs fight over the limb, snarling at each other like dogs.

My stomach sinks to the floor. But not from the foul, putrid act I see from across the room. No, it's much worse than that. It's the feeling of failure that sickens me.

And I'm now absolutely positive that this woman's head is completely fucked.

And none of us are getting out of here alive.

23

Janet Webber has gone.

For now, at least. Who knows when she'll bless us with her presence again. For once I'd happily pray for Necs to burst through the front door and storm the house. At least she'd be the first to go—maybe rip off her fucking head. It might take them a little more time to find us down here. At least we'd be safe. Well, not exactly safe. Not with these bloody ropes tied around us. So tight. My hands and feet have lost virtually all sensation. I feel they're gonna go black and drop off any minute. I've tried biting through them but had zero effect. And there's nothing for me to rub them against.

How the *hell* did I end up here? In this dungeon? I look over to Sammy, but I can't see him. Just a silhouette. Janet was kind enough to knock off the light before she left. The room is in darkness, apart from the weak glow from the staircase bulb. I can only hear her family chomp down on the last of the Cleaner's corpse. I very much doubt the poor bastard will turn. Can't see there being much of him left even if the disease did manage to get into his bloodstream.

The thought of her dead family so near to me—to Sammy—fills me with a foreboding that I've never felt before. Even with a job like mine, I never thought that he would ever be so close to danger; that I'd be so powerless to protect him. And what if those ropes snap? What chance do we have to defend ourselves against an attack? Absolutely none. Am I meant to just take her word that she's tied them up tight? The word of a fucking maniac?

At least it's too dark for Sammy to see them. And more importantly—they can't see him.

Poor little boy.

Don't know what time is it. Feels late. Must be night by now. Got to be. The tranq would have knocked me out for a good six or seven hours. *Easily.* Shame they don't work as well on Necs.

So thirsty. Can't remember the last time I drank something. I think maybe over in Edith's house.

Oh my God: *Edith.*

It feels like a lifetime ago. But it was only yesterday. Or was it the day before? Can't remember. This whole mess feels like one, everlasting nightmare. And now that I've found Sammy, it should be over.

But it's far from over.

"You okay, Sammy?" I whisper to him, not wanting to rile up the Necs. "Are you hurt at all?"

"I'm okay, Daddy," he replies, his voice quiet but hoarse. He needs water.

I hold off another dose of tears from the sound of his voice. Can't show him how scared I am. How lost I feel. Have to show him how happy I am to be near him. Have to let him believe that he's safe.

Even if it is a lie.

"Did the lady tie the ropes too tight around your hands, Sammy?" I ask him.

"A little, Daddy."

"Does it hurt?"

He shakes his head.

I force a smile, even though I'm sure he can't see it. "Good boy, Sammy. You're a brave little soldier. When we get out of here, I'll take you wherever you want to go. I promise."

"With Mammy?"

My stomach churns as I hear his words. I can't answer. Tears get the better of me. I try to hide the sound of despair by burying my mouth into my sleeve, but all it does is soften the noise. I try to gather myself, but can't. How the hell do I tell him the truth? It's impossible. He's too young. He's only four. No four-year-old should have to go through all this *shit*. It's not right. It's not *fucking right!*

"Mammy's still in work, boy," I lie, somehow containing my grief.

"When will she be back?" Sammy asks.

"We'll see her soon, boy. When she finishes."

"Okay, Daddy."

His groggy, weak sounding voice causes me to clench my fists. How can Janet do this to him? He's only a child. What kind of person could tie up a little boy down a grotty, old basement?

Crazy *bitch!*

I'm gonna fucking kill her!

I tug hard on the ropes, but they don't budge. And my skin is too swollen around them for any movement.

"How are we going to get out of here?" I ask

Sandra. "We have to think of something. I'm not gonna die down here. None of us are. There's gotta be a way. She's just one bloody woman."

"We can't," Sandra replies, coldly.

"What do you mean *we can't*? Of course we can."

"Why do you think the Cleaner was passed out next to you?"

"Don't know. Lack of water?"

"No. He managed to bite through his ropes. But she caught him. Smashed him over the head with a metal pole. And just let him bleed all over the floor. That's why the ropes are so tight—she's not gonna risk anyone else trying to escape."

"*Jesus Christ.* How can she be so deluded? I mean, thinking she's found the cure. She's completely lost her mind!" Sighing loudly, I try to calm down. "Has she always been such a psycho?"

"No. Well, not really. A little weird, maybe. Her and her family have always kept to themselves. You know, nothing *that* strange. Just," she shrugs, "odd."

"Jesus. I had no idea anyone in Crandale could be capable of such a thing. Christ, I saw her the other day. She was crossing the road. In the same bloody dressing gown. She stepped out right in front of me. She seemed weird then, but nothing like this. I'd never have guessed she'd turned out to be some crazy lunatic. Not in a million years."

"I know. I've known her for twenty years. Not like friends, though, just neighbours. And those poor kids—keeping them like this. It's not right. My son used to play with her boy all the time. Didn't think anything of it. Can't believe what it's done to her—she's really lost it."

"Look, Sandra, we have to get out of here. There's gotta be a way. We have to think of something. *Anything*. I'm not gonna let anything happen to Sammy. He's just a kid. He shouldn't be here. None of us should. We can't be so close to those Necs. It's too dangerous."

"I don't think they can move, Rob. I think they've been down here for a while."

"What if they bite through *their* ropes? What then? Every noise we make provokes them—gets them *angry*. We need to go now."

"I don't see how. She's completely nuts, but she knows how to tie a rope tight. I've tried and tried to wriggle free, but it's impossible."

"What about breaking this pipe?" I ask, yanking the rope hard. "Maybe if we pull it hard enough we could snap it. Or find something we can use to cut them? Something sharp? Must be something lying around here."

"There's nothing. Not a thing. She's made sure of it. I've looked. Not even a bloody paperclip."

"What about if we burn the ropes?"

"With what?"

"Janet's got a lighter in her pocket. I saw it when I came in. She gave me a cigarette."

"How are we supposed to get it?"

I ponder for moment. "*Okay*, the next time she comes down here we'll—"

"Rob, the next time she comes down here she'll be feeding me to her bloody family."

"Do you smoke, Sandra?"

"Yeah. Sometimes. Why?"

"Then you can ask her for a cigarette. One last smoke before you die."

"She won't even give us food and water. Do you seriously think she's gonna care about my smoking habit?"

"She might. You never know. We have to at least try. Once she hands you the lighter, I'll distract her—then you slip it to me."

"It's not gonna work, Rob. It's stupid. If she's down here, then she's here to drag me over to her family. You won't have *time* to burn through your ropes. There's no way."

"Then we have to get her down here *before* she plans to kill you."

"How are we supposed to do that?"

"We call her."

"We call her?"

"Yeah. What's wrong with that?"

"Well, what are you gonna say to her when she comes? *If* she comes?"

"I'll tell her that Sammy needs water. Say that he's sick. You said yourself she's been giving him some."

"Yeah, but…"

"You thirsty, Sammy?" I ask him. "Daddy get some water for you?"

He doesn't reply.

"Sammy? You thirsty?"

Still no reply.

An electric shock of panic shunts me. I'm about to scream at him. Call his name at the top of my voice. Oblivious to the Necs opposite me. Unconcerned about Janet upstairs.

But then Sandra gently shushes me, and whispers. "He's all right, Rob. He's just sleeping. Don't worry. He's fine."

A loud sigh of relief settles my nerves. But only for a moment. Sammy may be asleep for now, but it's only a matter of time before Janet—

"Look, Rob, this is a bad idea. Even if she *does* give me a cigarette, the chances of her handing the lighter over are slim to none. She'd most likely just light it herself. It's hopeless, Rob. I'm sorry—but it is."

"Then what the fuck are we supposed to do?" I snap. "Sit down here and wait to die?"

"No. But we have to think of something better. She may have lost her mind, but she's not stupid. And that's what makes her so bloody dangerous."

"No, what makes her so dangerous is having

that huge meat cleaver and tranquiliser gun. Plus, her dead family is sat opposite us."

"Look, there must be *something* we can tell her. Maybe something to do with her family. Maybe tell her you know a way to cure them."

"I thought you said she wasn't stupid? Only a complete *idiot* would believe something like that."

"Yes, but it's worth a shot. At least you could say that it's only a theory. Even say that you don't believe it yourself. Come on, Rob, think of something. You must have *something* from your job you could use to convince her."

"Maybe. But what's the point? I've already told her that there's no cure."

"I know that, but—"

"Well…there might be *something* I could say. Don't know if she'll buy it, though."

"What is it?"

"Well, there's a crashed Cleaner van just up the road from here. And I bet it's *loaded* with antiviral shots. So what if I told her that there's a theory that if a Nec is showing any signs of human behaviour, then maybe a huge dosage of the shot could reverse the effects of Necro-Morbus. She already said that her daughter's been showing signs of improvement. I mean, she *could* buy it—just."

"That's not bad, Rob. Not bad at all. And you could say that it doesn't work for every Nec, just a few. You know, to make it sound more believable."

"Yeah. And I could say that it's unlikely that the shot will bring them back completely, but close, depending on the level of necrosis."

"That's great, Rob. So maybe you could say that you'll go out to the van and get them."

"Wait. She's never gonna let me leave."

"She will if she still has Sammy. She knows that you'd never abandon your own son."

"Yeah, maybe. It could work," I say, optimistically. "She might believe it—it almost sounds true even to *me*."

"I know. And when she unties you, Rob—"

"I'll smash her fucking skull in."

"Well, I *was* gonna suggest you try and grab the gun from her—but your way sounds better."

I smile. Can't believe I have one in me, especially down here—especially today. But I do.

And the very notion of an escape plan feels nerve-racking, but at the same time slightly exciting. To create an opportunity to have one up on that psycho *bitch* sounds pretty fucking good to me.

Don't think I've ever hated anyone as much. Every time I think of that thick red hair, that grubby white dressing gown, I feel my blood pressure rising; almost bursting at the seams.

"We doing this or what?" Sandra says, excitement in her tone.

Or absolute terror.

"Okay. Let's call her then," I say, reluctantly, even though I try to mask it.

"JANET!" Sandra screams at the top of her voice. The noise startles the three Necs. Waiting for the sound of footsteps to come down the stairs, I recoil, unsure of which disturbs me more: the barking corpses opposite—or Janet *fucking* Webber.

Pointing my ear up towards the ceiling, I hear a faint thumping sound, and the creaking of floorboards. My stomach feels sick with apprehension as I wait for the door to open and the light to come on. What kind of mood will she be in?

For all we know, the very sound of her name is enough for her to start hacking at us with the meat cleaver.

Perhaps a minute passes. Maybe less. Hard to tell. Then another, before Sandra shouts: "JANET! WE NEED TO TALK!"

This time the vibrations through the floorboards fill the room, as if Janet is pissed off, stomping down heavily on the floor. The Necs seem even more agitated. The sound reaches the basement door. Turning towards it, I see Janet as she comes stamping hard down each step until she reaches the bottom. By the time she flicks on the main light switch, my body is almost in spasm at the sight of her; grasping the meat cleaver in her hand as predicted.

My enthusiasm to feed her this bullshit story has suddenly vanished.

"Yes. What do you want?" Janet says; gently shushing her diseased family like a crying baby.

"Rob's got something to tell you," Sandra says. "Don't you, Rob?" Turning to me.

Thanks for that.

"Yeah. I need to tell you about a medical theory about a possible cure."

"What are you talking about?" Janet asks, scowling at me, her eyes piercing as if the very mention of another cure is ludicrous.

"It's just a theory. Nothing more. And I don't really believe it myself. But there's always a chance. Always hope."

"Thought you didn't think there *was* a cure? You told me that my family was dead. Why the sudden change of heart? Trying to bullshit me, is it?"

"Look, I've already *told you* that I don't believe it—it's just a theory. One of hundreds. But I also told you that I don't believe that feeding your family is gonna cure them either. And that hasn't exactly deterred you. So what have you got to lose?"

"All right then, Rob—*tell me*. What's this new cure of yours?"

"*Okay.* There's a theory: if the infected body is showing any signs of humanity—memories, moments of calm—there's a chance that if you inject them with an extremely high dosage of antiviral, then it *could* reverse the effects. Maybe not fully, but enough to bring back some basic human functions, like speech and control of aggression."

Janet looks at me; an expression of distrust yet showing signs of intrigue.

Have I convinced her?

Maybe.

She glances down at her family again, as they groan and dribble like three dosed up lunatics. What's she thinking? Seems like she's contemplating it; too hard to call it though.

But then I feel that excitement bubble up again when she says: "Even if I did believe you, I don't have any antiviral shots. No one has. So your so-called *cure* is useless to me anyway."

"I can get you some," I reply, my enthusiasm restored.

Janet smiles sarcastically. "Oh yeah, and how are you meant to do that? Make a little trip through the barricades, down to the Doctor's office, is it? Get a prescription? You think I'm a bloody moron?"

"*No.* I don't think you're a moron. There's a Cleaner van just a little up the street. It's crashed. I tried to save the driver yesterday, but we got ambushed. They killed him. Inside the van, I saw hundreds of antiviral shots. Boxes of them. Enough for your son, daughter, *and* your husband."

Very subtly, Janet nods. "I've seen it. I saw it crash. It almost ran me down."

"*See*. I'm not bullshitting you, I promise. Let me run up the hill and grab a few boxes. And I'll be back in less than five minutes. Easily."

Janet says nothing, as if mulling it over. Can't lose her now. Have to keep pushing it. "You know I can't run out on you. I'd never leave Sammy on his own. Not down here. *Please, Janet.* We have to at least try. For the sake of your family. If this works— even if it's just one of your family—this will change everything. This could be the breakthrough the world's been waiting for. And this would have been all worth it. All the death. All the suffering. All the sacrifice. All for this: The *real* cure."

Staring deep into Janet's eyes, I search for a glimmer of humanity. A part of her that existed long before all this madness started. A part of her that would rather believe my screwed up story than her psychotic idea.

While I'm lost in her gaze, praying that she doesn't start to pick out the gaping holes in my story, I see something—something that I never thought I'd see down here.

A tear.

Need to exploit this now. Have to keep plugging. For all our sakes. "Just let me do this for you and your family. I need this to work just as much as you do. *Please*."

Janet wipes the tear away with the sleeve from her meat-cleaver hand. The image is disturbing—but hopeful. "All right," she says, nodding. "But *she* has to go. Not you." She points the meat cleaver over to Sandra.

I turn to Sandra in shock. On the one hand, I can't believe that she actually bought my bullshit story—and on the other, that she's picked Sandra to go. Why? And how the *hell* is she meant to overpower Janet when she's untied? She's starving, and clearly weak. Plus, she's half the size of Janet. She wouldn't stand a chance out there.

But that's exactly why.

Janet ain't taking any risks. I could take her

down if she unties me. The last time, she surprised me with a dart in the shoulder—this time I'd be fucking ready for the lanky cunt!

And she knows it!

"That's fine," Sandra says, grudgingly. "I'm happy to go instead of Rob."

"No. That's not a good idea," I say to Janet. "She won't last five minutes outside with all those Necs. The van could be *crawling* with them. It's better if it's me."

"No," Janet replies, conviction in her tone, "she's going, and that's that. And I know she'll be back. She'd never leave without your little boy. Not in a million years."

"She's right," Sandra says. "I wouldn't. I'd rather *die* than see you harm a hair on his head."

"See," Janet says, half-smiling.

"How's she meant to defend herself out there?" I ask.

Janet walks over to Sandra, goes down on one knee, and then starts to cut through her ropes with the meat cleaver. "Don't underestimate her, Robert; I'm sure she'll be fine. She's resourceful."

Sandra looks at me with terror in her eyes. She knows as well as I do that we have to be careful not to protest her decision. It's too risky. She could take it back at any second. Have to let it play out and pray to God that Sandra can think of something— maybe push Janet down the stairs on the way up. Hopefully, she'll split her fucking head open on the way down, smash her face on the washing machine. And then maybe she could drop that generator on her.

See how she likes that!

Sandra's ropes finally split open and drop to the floor. I watch as Sandra glares down at her burned and swollen skin. She's been down here even longer than I have, and already mine are torn up pretty bad. Hers must be agony.

Janet backs away, pointing the meat cleaver at Sandra's chest. Sandra tries to stand, but her knees give way. I reach up with my hands to catch her but can't. Using the wall for support, she tries again, this time managing to get laboriously to her feet. Janet has moved back to the opposite wall, next to her daughter.

"You all right?" I ask Sandra.

She nods, and then forces a smile through cracked lips. "Don't worry about me, Rob. I'll be fine. I'm as tough as old boots."

Not sure what she's thinking. I wish I could read her thoughts right now; find out her plan of action. That's if she even has one. For all I know, she's going straight to the van to look for the antiviral shots—even though there's a possibility that she might not even find one, let alone bloody boxfuls.

"Where are you going, Sandra?" I hear Sammy ask; his voice croaky, half-asleep.

Turning to him, I see that he's started to push himself back into a seated position against the wall. "Don't worry, Sammy," I tell him. "She's just going outside to help Janet with something. She won't be long."

"I'll be right back, Sammy," Sandra turns to say. "Keep your Dad company for me, will you? I'll be back before you know it." She then carries on forward towards the stairs, limping painfully with every step.

As she passes the three Necs, I watch in horror

as Janet swings the meat cleaver; slicing into Sandra's left knee. Sandra screams out in agony as her legs buckle. She then hits the hard floor, her face grimacing with pain.

"THERE'S ONLY ONE FUCKING CURE!" Janet yells hard into her ear. "AND THAT'S YOU!"

Sandra tries to stand up, but Janet pushes her onto her side with her foot. Suddenly, Janet's husband reaches forward and takes hold of Sandra's hair. Her screams of panic are drowned out by the growls of the Necs as she's dragged into the middle of them. I shuffle frantically over to Sammy, hoping to block out the sight. But it's too late. Sandra's body is devastated with bite marks by the time I reach him. Burying Sammy's face into my chest, I just about manage to hinder any further revulsion. But only for him. The Necs pass her helpless body around like hyenas with their prey. I fight off an urge to vomit as I watch Sandra's eyes close when her stomach is clawed open, and her intestines are hauled out like thick, brown cable, and eaten.

All I can do now is pray that she's already dead; that her suffering is over.

•

At least she won't become one of those *things*. Thank God for that.

But only that.

I lightly shush Sammy's grief, trying to sooth his anguish like I would after a bump on the head, or a nasty fall. But I can still hear his screams even with his mouth covered. His cries for Sandra. His friend. No one should ever have to see such a thing. Something so earth shattering. So heart-breaking.

So loathsome.

"*I don't wanna play this game anymore*," Sammy weeps, his words barely audible. "*I just wanna go home, Daddy.*"

"It'll be over soon," I say, as a censored rage builds in the pit of my stomach. A rage that will only vanish when Sammy and I are free of this basement. And when I've smashed that *bitch's head against the wall!*

Only then.

"I'm sorry he had to see that, Rob," Janet says, her voice cold, her eyes glazed over with quiet madness. "I know he was fond of her. She was a good woman, and I'm sorry it had to be her down here. I wish it could've been someone else." She kneels down next to her daughter, reaches up, and then tenderly strokes Sophie's long, red hair. But the fact that the Nec isn't taking a bite out of her hand has nothing to do with love. Nothing to do with a cure. It's the simple fact that the Nec's mouth is already full. Full to the brim with Sandra's flesh. But from the smile on Janet's face as her hand runs up and down her daughter's head, her sick and twisted delusion has undoubtedly taken over. And there's nothing me or anyone could ever say to bring her back.

"You okay, Sammy?" I whisper down to him.

He doesn't reply. And his silence only heightens my bitterness and hatred for Janet. "You're *sick!*" I say to her, spitting my words out like poison. "You're just some psychotic *screw-up* that always gets what she wants. Happy to step on anyone to get somewhere. That's who you are, Janet. And now it's made you into a sick murderer."

"If I *were* a sick murderer," Janet replies, still stroking her daughter's knotted hair, "I would have let my family tear *you* limb from limb instead. And not her."

"Then why didn't you?"

"Because I wouldn't do that to your son. Not yet anyway. Not if I can help it. He needs his father."

"So just let us go then—and this can all be over."

"I can't let you go. I have to think about my family."

"Is this how you'd like your family to remember you? Killing a helpless little boy? Is it? For God's sake, Janet, he's just a baby. He shouldn't be here. *Christ*, he's already lost so much. Are you really gonna do this to him? After everything else?"

Janet moves her hand away from her daughter's head, and then stands. "Not if I don't have to."

"What's *that* supposed to mean?"

"He's only here as a precaution. The last thing I want to do is kill him. But my family is sick. They need to be fed—or they'll die. One by one. And I can't have that. I just can't. So, as long as I can find someone new to feed them—someone else from outside maybe—the better chance he has of staying alive. And that's a promise."

I shake my head in disbelief. "That's ridiculous. How are you supposed to find anyone else? Crandale's been abandoned."

"I found *you*, didn't I?"

"No, you didn't find me. I came looking for you. Remember?"

Janet takes a loving glance at her decaying family as they continue to devour Sandra. "I'd do anything for my family. Absolutely anything." She then flips the main light switch, and the basement turns to darkness again. "You of all people should know that."

"Janet! Wait! *Please!*"

But my desperate pleas are lost in the sound of heavy footsteps going up the stairs.

I can still feel the judders of turmoil as Sammy continues to sob into my chest. But at least he's close to me. At least I can touch him; smell him.

And at least the darkness has masked the hideous sight of Sandra's ravaged body. I start to hum a tune to him, hoping to soothe his suffering, like I used to when he was a baby; when he couldn't sleep. Anna always had the gift of getting him off to sleep. But not me. I always had to resort to making up silly songs about his day, or walking up and down the stairs.

A hum turns into a song as the sound of gnawing increases.

Anything to block out the noise.

24

A sudden shockwave of panic hits me.

Can't believe I fell asleep. The room is still in darkness; impossible to know what time it is. None of us has a watch, and there certainly isn't a clock down here. Could be a bright, sunny afternoon, or the middle of the night. I feel as if I've spent a day on a plane and I'm jetlagged. So disorientated. So exhausted. And my neck and lower back is in agony. I shuffle a little and move my head side to side, but it does nothing to ease the pain.

I can still feel and hear Sammy as he sleeps next to me; his face pressed against my chest. I pray that he didn't truly understand what happened to Sandra. That he thought—

My God, I don't know *what* he thought.

He must be starving. When was the last time he ate something? Yesterday? The day before?

Fuck!

Can't let us end up like Sandra. No bloody way. Can't risk anymore stupid plans. Janet's not an idiot. She'll see through any more lies.

Have to be smarter.

The image of Sandra's demise will be etched on my soul for the rest of my life—that's if I ever get out of this *stinking basement*. The chances of Janet finding someone else for her family to feed on are slim. And even if it *did* buy him another day or two, what kind of life is that? Just waiting to die. How long could he hold out before someone rescued him? And what if they didn't? What if she just keeps him down here for years? Just keeps him tied up for all that time? Her family is just gonna get more rotten every day—and hungrier with every hour that passes. Surely she'll have to realise that there *is* no bloody cure—her family is *dead*.

I need to kill that bitch today.

The pipe rattles as I tug on my ropes. I'm sure I can break this rusty piece of shit. I tug on it again, this time with double the force. I hear the sound of rust fragments falling to the ground. Must be pretty worn. I can do this. *Fuck the ropes.* I can still kill her even with my wrists tied. And when she's dead, I can just hop out of here.

Have to be quiet though. Who knows how

much she can hear from up there? For all I know she's got a bloody baby monitor strapped to her, listening to every sound we make.

I carefully move Sammy's sleeping head away from my chest, trying not to wake him, and then rest it on the floor. Twisting around, I can feel the ropes burn and dig into my wrists, cutting deep into my already suppurated and scorched flesh. I close my eyes tight to block out the searing pain as I place my feet onto the wall, trying to gain leverage.

Come on, Rob. You can do this. You can fucking *do this!*

I brace for a moment to ready myself, and then take hold of the rope tightly with both hands, before pulling on it as hard as I can. The pain in my wrists is unbearable. I can feel my strength start to fade already, my grip on the rope loosening.

No. Come one, Rob. You've got to do this. For Sammy. For Anna. A sudden burst of energy fills my aching body. Pulling with everything I have, I listen out for the pipe, hoping to hear a cracking sound. But nothing. I keep tugging; teeth grinding hard, trying to swallow the pain.

Please break. Please, God, let this be it!

Please…

But before my prayers get answered, before I'm embraced by sweet freedom, my body surrenders to defeat. I collapse against the floor, exhausted. Too tired even to scream out in agony from my torn up wrists.

I've failed.

Failed myself. And what's worse, I've failed Sammy.

Overcome with frustration, I start to cry. I try not to but can't control my emotions; can't control the hopelessness of the situation. The fact that even after finding Sammy, I still can't protect him—*still can't get him home.*

God I wish I could turn back the clock. Even if it was after Anna got infected. Just go back to the morning before I left for work. I could have stayed and had breakfast with them. Watched cartoons with him—like a normal father—instead of racing out the door, as usual, to get to some overworked, underpaid job. For Christ's sake, if I'd spent half the time I took to moan about how hard my job was, how difficult my life is, then maybe I could've used that time to play with him a little more. Or tell Anna how much I loved her—how much I *needed* her.

How thankful I was for every minute she gave me.

And now look where I am—rotting away in some psycho's basement, waiting to die.

God help me!

"Don't cry, Daddy," I hear Sammy whisper to me.

His sweet voice pulls me out of my despair. I sit up and slide back over to him. Squeezing up as close as I can, I look down at him with a smile. "I'm not crying, Sam. Daddy was just laughing to himself."

"Why were you laughing?"

"I was thinking about how *silly* you are."

"*You're* silly, Daddy," he replies, playfully.

"Oh, I am, am I? You *cheeky-little-monkey*." I reach over and tickle him. My fingers barely function, but I still manage to get a strained chuckle from him.

I almost forget where I am.

I gently stroke the top of his hand, where his

ropes are tied. Prodding with my finger, I try to feel how tight they are. Maybe she hasn't bothered to tie them so well. Maybe he could wriggle his hands out.

And what then? He unties me and we ride out like cowboys?

No, that's stupid. He'd never be able to get me out of these. And I couldn't exactly get him to make a run for it on his own. What if he got caught? She might drag him back down here; feed him to the Necs—just to piss me off. No, it's too risky. Even if she did mean what she said about keeping him alive, there's no telling what else she might do to him— especially pissed off.

Forget about it.

"Did you have a nice sleep?" I ask him.

"No, Daddy."

"Why's that, Sammy?"

"My head hurts."

"Where does it hurt? All over?"

"Yes. And I need to go to the toilet again."

"Okay, Sammy. Did you pee yourself before?"

"Yes."

"All right. You may have to do the same again.

But don't worry about it. We won't be down here much longer. I promise. Daddy's gonna take you home soon. Okay?"

"Okay, Daddy."

Tension builds up in my body again. I start to fidget from anxiety. I can feel my chest tightening.

Need to get him some food and water right now.

"JANET!" I scream at the top of my voice. "WE NEED YOU!" The words seem broken and stressed, so I cough loudly to clear my throat, and then cry out again. "JANET! WE NEED YOU DOWN HERE—RIGHT NOW!"

The Necs begin to stir, yowling in the darkness like disrupted beasts.

I hear the creaking of floorboards above me, and then the basement door opening. The floor vibrates as heavy footsteps come trudging down the stairs. I shuffle even tighter to Sammy, trying to sit slightly in front of him. Don't know what kind of mood she's in. Don't know how late it is. I might have woken her up at four o'clock in the morning.

The main light comes on. It blinds me as I half-close my eyes. When they adjust to the brightness, I see Janet standing next to the far wall.

And then I see Sandra. What's left of her, anyway. The Necs have managed to devour almost her entire body, apart from a few bones and lumps of muscle. The sight of her family sends a shudder of repulse through my body; their greasy, lifeless hair; their clothes soaked through with blood and bile; their brownish-grey skin, withered like a ninety-year old; and teeth, still gnawing the flesh around pieces of bone. I glance down at Sammy as I feel his body tense up, clearly terrified by their unsightly appearance.

I don't know what he thinks they are. Maybe nothing. Just a man and his two children tied down in the basement like him. Just as much a victim as we are. But their grotesque features are enough to make anyone frightened—even if he doesn't understand.

But I know exactly what they are; what they're capable of.

And it turns my stomach.

"So, what is it?" Janet impatiently asks me.

"We need some water," I reply, my voice filled with conviction like a terrorist making demands to a negotiator. "My son isn't going to last much longer without something to eat or drink. And he'll be no good to you then. If you truly believe that your family need to feed on us to survive, then you'd better start looking after your food supply. We're no good to you dead. You said yourself they only eat fresh meat. So I want some water and something to eat right now."

Janet doesn't say anything. She then turns and stares down at her family as they lazily graze on Sandra's remains.

"You're right," she says, still peering down at them. "You're absolutely right. I need to look after you better."

I can't believe my ears. Finally, I can hear the voice of an almost rational person. "And we need to use the toilet. Sammy's gonna get an infection if he pees himself again. We both are. It's not a lot to ask—a little dignity."

Janet looks over to me, shaking her head. "You think I'm stupid. I'd never let you go to the bloody toilet. You'd try to escape the moment I untie you. You've proven that I can't trust you, Rob."

"No, I wouldn't try anything. Not with the chance of a meat cleaver in the back of the head. Or another round from the tranq gun. It's too risky. And besides, if you let me go first, then I'm not likely to do anything stupid. Not while you still have Sammy."

Janet falls silent again, as if mulling over a decision. After a few seconds, she shakes her head. "No. It's too risky. I can't have you walking 'round upstairs. If I had a bathroom down here, then I would. But it's upstairs, so forget it. You can both piss and shit on the floor. It ain't gonna kill you."

"Please, Janet," I plead. "You don't have to worry. At least let Sammy go. He's not exactly gonna do anything. *Please.*"

Sighing loudly, she scans the room, and then walks over to Malcolm. There is a shelf directly above him, with a plastic bucket at the centre. Reaching over him to grab it, I watch as the Nec slouches forward to bite her. She sees this and moves away quickly. "It's no good," she says, leaving the bucket on the shelf. "I'll get you some food and water—but that's it."

I'm desperate to bargain a little more, but can't risk her changing her mind about the water. Can't push her. I'm in no position to call any shots.

Janet takes a glance at her family, smiles and then disappears back up the stairs.

The light is still on. Noticing my bloodied and seared wrists, I nearly heave from the sight. So instead I turn to Sammy; his face is dirty; his lips are dry. Scanning his body, I see a large wet stain around the groin area of his pyjamas. I shake my head in disgust—disgust that anyone could be so cruel to a child.

Poor kid. I hope to *God* he doesn't remember this when he's older.

Older.

The thought of him missing out on a future makes me nauseous. How could I let this happen to him? How could I let him endure such torture? And literally right on our doorstep? How could I have been so careless? I'm his father for Christ's sake. It's my *job* to look out for him; keep him safe. Keep him away from lunatics like Janet *fucking* Webber!

I look over at the Necs. The daughter and father are leaning back against the wall, eyes half-closed, as if exhausted and sated from the feast. Janet's son is still rummaging around in a pool of blood and a concoction of fluids, still searching for something else to eat. Somehow, I pity them all. Maybe it's the sight of their wasted, emaciated bodies; their relentless need to eat; the fact that they're prisoners down here just like us. I can't help it. I know that the last thing I should be feeling is pity. But with Janet upstairs, believing that giving a captive four-year-old a glass of water is somehow charitable—I know *damn well* who the real monster is.

"I want to go home, Daddy," Sammy tells me. "I don't feel good."

"Not long now, Sam. I promise. Daddy's gonna get you home soon. And then we can play with your toys. Maybe watch a cartoon. How does that sound?"

"Okay, Daddy." He leans forward and kisses my hand. "Will Mammy be there too?"

My heart sinks to the floor.

The nausea returns and I close my eyes. "Of course she will, boy."

I pull him close and kiss his forehead, swallowing the angst like bitter medicine.

I listen to the sound of footsteps above me as Janet rustles around, hopefully making good on her promise. I don't hold out much hope of her changing her mind about letting us go, but food and water is a start. Maybe I just have to chip away at her good side. One step at a time. Try to get on her wavelength. Or close enough.

But how long have I got? What if there *is* no time to chip away? Can't let her take me, not in front of Sammy. If I knew he'd be safe, then I could handle it. *Just.* But the idea of him being left all alone in the same room as those rotting Necs is un*thinkable*.

The basement door bursts open. My body tightens with every footstep I hear coming down the stairs.

"There you go," Janet says, holding a plastic bottle of water and a small bag of crisps. "This should hold you both." She walks over to us and drops the items into my lap. "You can share. I ain't wasting any more food on you. Got to keep my supplies up. There's no predicting how long we'll be here before this is all over."

I open the crisps and hand the packet over to Sammy. "I take it by *we* you mean you and your family, yeah?" I ask her.

She walks over to her son and kneels. "Yes," she replies, reaching out to touch his ankle. Just as she's about to make contact, the Nec suddenly comes alive with rage and snaps his jaws down towards her hand. She pulls it away, broken teeth missing her exposed flesh by a centimetre. She quickly shuffles back, out of grabbing distance.

"See, Rob," she says, her voice clearly trying to mask her terror, "Jack's got a few more feedings before he's placid again. Not like Sophie." She looks over to her comatose daughter and smiles. "She's always been the easiest child. Never a peep out of her. But Jack, well, he's a different story altogether. He's always had a bit of a temper on him. But I suppose that's being sixteen for you. Teenagers *aye:* never happy." She glances at her husband. "He gets it from his father. He's always had a bit of a temper on him. *Oh, you wouldn't wanna catch him on a bad day. I can tell you.* But he's a good man. *Firm,* but fair." She touches his right leather shoe. The Nec doesn't respond. "And that's why I love him—in spite of his flaws."

I open the bottle of water, take a small taste, and then hand it over to Sammy. "Just a little sip now, Sammy," I whisper to him. "Save the rest for later." He nods his head and then gulps down a huge mouthful, leaking some onto his pyjamas.

Even though every droplet of water could mean the difference between life and death, I can't help but smile a little inside as it runs down his chin. He hands the bottle back to me, so I screw the cap back on, and then set the water down to my right side. I let him finish the packet of crisps. I think about rationing them, but there're so little of them in the bag that I don't bother. What's the point? Let him have this little pleasure.

My stomach aches with hunger, but I push the pain to one side. I can handle it. I've gone without food before. It's just mind over matter. *A healthy detox*. Nothing more.

As long as Sammy's all right, I'd happily endure a lifetime of it.

"So tell me, Janet," I ask her. "Where did you find Sammy? Did you just *snatch him* from my wife?"

Still kneeling, Janet turns to me, shaking her head. "No. I didn't *snatch him*. I didn't have to." She looks at Sammy and beams. "I saved him."

"What are you talking about? Saved him from what?"

"I found him sat in your wife's car, on his own. He was just sitting there, still strapped into the car seat."

"And where was Anna?"

Janet shrugs her shoulders. "There was no one else. Just a few wandering Necs. I took care of them, brought them down with the tranquiliser gun. Then I just got him inside as fast as I could."

"You should have left him there," I say with venom. "He would have been better off."

"Don't talk rot! They would have eaten him in a matter of seconds."

"Not with the door shut. Necs can't open

bloody doors."

"No, but they can smash a bloody window," she replies, sarcastically. "They're pretty good at that."

I shake my head in loathing. "Maybe. But he'd still be better off than down here." I glance at him as he crunches the last few crisps. "So how long was it?"

"How long was what?"

"Before you dragged him down the basement to meet the family?"

"Maybe a few hours. Couldn't risk him drawing any attention to the house. Plus, I needed him as a bargaining tool for Sandra and the Cleaner. Needed to give them a reason to stay."

"No. You gave them a reason to *kill you*."

"Well, it worked for Sandra. The very *notion* of any harm coming to him kept her in line. *Most of the time*. Not so much the other one, though. He was happy to push me, trying to call my bluff. Not a thought for your little boy. Selfish, really. Don't you think?"

"I doubt it. You talk as if *he* was to blame—but it was *you* who put us in this situation. No one else."

Janet stands up and walks over to Sophie. She carefully drops to one knee, reaches forward, and then starts to caress her daughter's hair again. The Nec doesn't flinch; it doesn't seem to even register the contact. Eyes barely open, in some kind of a trance. Most likely preserving her energy.

Until the next feed.

"Well, you've still got him, haven't you?" Janet says, eyes locked on her dead child. "He's still *him*, isn't he?" She shakes her head. "You may *think* you've got it bad. You think that seeing your child tied by his hands and wrists is the worst thing a father could witness. But you have no idea what real pain is. The pain of watching your entire family rot in front of your very eyes. Watching them ignore you. Being unable even to touch your own son!" She turns to me, eyes filled with angry tears. "At least you have that! Be thankful!"

"Janet, I know what you're going through. I understand your pain. I feel it every day. I felt it with Anna. The pain of her not recognising me. Seeing her skin like that. Her eyes empty. I know what it feels like. Anna was everything to me. She was funny, loving—would do anything for anyone. Without a second thought. And the perfect mother. And to see all that disappear was—"

I have to stop. It's too much.

But too hard to repress the memory of her death.

Too clear in my head.

The furnace.

The screams.

I battle hard to stop myself from tearing up again.

It's just...

"I know how she got sick," Janet tells me.

"*What?*"

"Your wife. Anna. I know how she got infected."

I can't believe what I'm hearing. I always thought that that knowledge was dead; burned away in the furnace with her. But now, this vile, putrid monster before me is about to tell me something that I'd rather not know. But there's a voice in my head, whispering to me.

It's telling me to let her speak.

"Malcolm's a delivery driver for the hospital. At it for a good twenty-five years. At *least*. Anyway, he had a call-out to pick up some blood samples from one of the nursing homes. There was only two staff on, and then they both were called to a resident's room. Malcolm had to wait by the nurse's station before he could leave. Think he had to get a signature or something. Anyway, maybe a minute or two passes and one of the nurses is screaming for help. So my husband runs as fast as he can to see what the problem is. When he gets to the room, one of the nurses is lying on the floor, and there's blood pouring out from her throat. Of course, Malcolm is in a state of shock. He's *frozen*. I mean, it's not something you're likely to see in a bloody old-people's home, now is it?"

Janet pauses to swallow before continuing. "Well, the other nurse is on the floor too, but she's still alive, screaming for him to pull this old man off her. I mean, this man's got to be well into his eighties, and he's somehow managed to overpower this nurse—who's at *least* half the man's age. Anyway, so Malcolm sprints over to the man and grabs his shoulders to drag him off her. Well, as he does, this old man takes a bite out of Malcolm's hand. Nothing that deep—but enough to break the skin. So Malcolm pushes the old man, and he falls back against the side of the bed. The nurse scrambles across the floor and out of the room, screaming blue bloody murder. The old man gets up onto his feet and then *lunges* for Malcolm. But luckily Malcolm manages to run out the door. And then he slams the door in the old man's face. Anyway, poor old Malcolm has to sit with this nurse for a good twenty minutes while he waits for the police to show up. Well, this policeman must have been an idiot or new to his job because he didn't think of calling those Cleaners. He just took this nurse and Malcolm's statements, then sent him on his way. Didn't even notice his hand. And thank God for *that*." Janet glances over to her husband and smiles with pride. "My bloody hero."

"So what's this got to do with Anna?" I ask, impatiently.

"I'm getting to that, Rob," she replies, shaking her head in annoyance. "So, anyway, Malcolm comes home, *completely* unaware that the old man was infected with Necro-Morbus. Christ, he even forgot he was bitten until I asked him about his hand when he got home. I mean, when he told me what happened, even *I* didn't click the old man had it. I thought he was just some senile idiot who just went nuts. We *both* did. Anyone would. But then during the night, Malcolm got a fever. A really bad one. I thought nothing of it at first, until I saw his hand. It'd all swollen up, blackened, and was oozing with pus. And it looked like it was spreading up his arm. I bandaged it up and gave him a few painkillers. But then we both looked at each other. And I'll never forget this until the day I die, but…we both knew what it was. And we both knew what was going to happen over the next few hours."

"So why didn't you take him to the hospital. They could have given him an antiviral shot."

"What, so someone like *you* could burn him in a bloody furnace? Not a fucking chance!"

"But it might have saved his life."

"It was too late for him. I couldn't risk it. And if it *were* too late then they would have taken him away from us. And I wasn't having any of that. *No bloody way*. Not with two kids that needed him." Janet wipes her teary eyes with the sleeve of her dressing gown, and then sniffs loudly. "Sophie was the first to be bitten. When he started to get aggressive, I tied Malcolm down here, but I forget to lock the door. Sophie wandered down. I'd told her that her Daddy was on holiday with his friend. Only Jack knew the truth."

"How long was he down here before she found him?"

"Not sure," she replies, shrugging her shoulders. "Maybe two weeks."

"*Jesus Christ*. Two weeks?"

Janet nods; her eyes filled with shame. "*I had to*. I even told her that he took the three dogs with him. I mean, I couldn't exactly tell her that I'd fed them to her father now, could I? She's only seven, for Christ's sake. I had to protect her from the truth." She looks at Sophie's tortured, shrivelled face and starts to sob uncontrollably. "*I'm so sorry, Sophie. I'm so sorry I couldn't protect you from this horrible disease!*"

The basement is silent for maybe a minute as

Janet tries to collect herself. "I'm sorry," she says. "Don't like to cry in front of the children. Don't like to show weakness around them. With everything that's happened, they need me to be the strong one now, more than ever."

"You don't have to tell me all the details, Janet. I know it's hard."

"It's all right. Need to tell someone. Got no one else to tell." She sniffs loudly and then lets out a long sigh. "Sophie thought her Daddy was just sitting against the wall. *And then...*" Janet covers her face with her hand, clearly holding back her anguish.

I almost feel sorry for her.

"So why didn't you take her straight to the hospital?" I ask. "Surely you had time with her?"

"There was no hope with Sophie. Malcolm had bitten her legs so deep, that when Jack found her, she was passed out on the basement stairs—bleeding to death. He dragged her up to the living room. I was out picking up supplies from town. By the time I walked through the door, Sophie had bitten off three of Jack's fingers."

Peeking over to her son, I notice his missing

fingers; the stumps all dried out and black.

"I'm sorry you had to go through that," I tell her, genuinely, even though it pains me to say.

She nods her head and smiles subtly. "Before I could even see to Jack—before I could even come to terms with the fact that Sophie had turned, I had to get her down to the basement—before she hurt anyone else. I dragged her body, kicking and screaming down the stairs. I just imagined that she was having one of her tantrums. I pretended that she'd been playing up and I had to drag her to her bedroom. It was the only way I could cope. The only way to get her to safety before anyone came knocking on the front door.

"After I tied her next to her father, I ran upstairs to check on Jack. He was sitting on the floor, up against the sofa, holding his bleeding hand, staring down at his three bitten-off fingers. It was horrible. *But fixable.* So I ran into the kitchen, grabbed a plastic container from the cupboard, then filled it with ice. I grabbed the first-aid kit and a towel and went back in to see Jack. He was in shock by this point, white as a sheet. Shaking. Not sure if it was just the shock of losing his fingers, or the shock of seeing his sister like that. By the time I got his coat from the kitchen, I knew he was infected. The wound was black and swollen. And it was spreading up into his wrist. I knew I didn't have long before…"

Janet takes in a huge breath of air, and then exhales loudly, as if struggling to keep it together. "I knew I had to at least try to get an antiviral shot for him, so I wrapped the towel over his hand, then rushed him out of the house and into my car. I drove as fast as I could to the hospital. But the traffic was a mess. Once I reached the city centre, it was chock-a-block. And Jack was getting woozy. His eyes kept rolling back. And he kept swearing at me, calling me *all* names, using words I've *never* heard come out of his mouth. It was horrible. I tried to tell him to calm down, to keep pressure on his hand. *But it was no use.* By the time I reached the hospital, the infection had spread up his entire left side. I slammed on the breaks and drove back home."

"Why would you *do* that? You could have *saved* him."

"No. It was too risky. I couldn't take the chance. They would have taken him away from me. And what's worse, they would have come for Malcolm and Sophie. There was too much to lose. You *know* how hit-and-miss those shots are. Even if you had one straightaway. Especially with bites."

I don't answer because she's right—it probably was too late for him. And they would have taken him away to be burned. And they would have definitely come for the rest of her family.

But at least then I wouldn't be in this mess.

"So how does Anna fit into all this?" I ask.

"When me and Jack pulled up outside the house, I struggled to get him out of the car. He could barely stand on his own two feet. I mean, he's a big, strong lad, and he weighs a *ton*. So your wife saw me struggling, and she came over to help. She asked me what was wrong with him, and I told her that he hurt himself playing rugby. As we got him to the front door, he coughed up some blood over Anna's face. I mean…she was a good woman. I've gotta say. She didn't even stop to wipe it off until Jack was safely inside the house. Can't fault her there. I really can't."

I feel sick.

This woman has taken *everything* from me. And for what? So she could have a few more days to watch her family rot? What kind of reason is that? No sane person would risk so much for so little in return. Surely the pain of seeing them like this is far greater than letting them die.

Does she even see the state they're in? Maybe she's blocked it out. Repressed it. It's possible.

She's crazy enough.

But why didn't Anna tell me? Why couldn't she have just mentioned that she might have swallowed infected blood? I could have helped her; could have driven her to the hospital. Didn't she *know* she was infected?

Maybe she forgot to say. Maybe there was never a good time. All I went on about was how tough my fucking job was. Did I even ask how her day went? Did I even ask how she was feeling? Probably not. Maybe if I had, she might have mentioned what happened. *Maybe I could have...*

"When I got Jack inside the living room," Janet

continues, "I left him to check on Malcolm and Sophie. I was only gone a minute or two. But by the time I got back upstairs, Jack was gone. He must have gone through the backdoor. Don't even know if he'd turned when he left—but he was turned when I eventually found him."

"How long was he out there for?"

"All night. I found him the next day. Well, I wasn't exactly the one who found him. After I'd driven 'round Crandale looking for him, the Cleaners were already here. I assume he killed a few people on the way to God knows where, otherwise, why else would they have come? They'd already brought him down with the tranquiliser gun, so I rammed them both with my car. Not sure if I killed them or not—didn't hang around to find out. I just grabbed a gun and dragged Jack into the back seat of the car before anyone saw me. Then just brought him here. Home. Where he belongs."

I shake my head, completely stunned by her words. "That's unbelievable. I had no *idea* what you've been through. No wonder you're so stressed."

Nodding, Janet turns to her family, her eyes filled with unconditional love. "But they're worth it. Every single one of them. Family is the most important thing in the world."

"I know. We've always been a close family. Not just Sammy and Anna. Mum and I are really close. Especially since my father died. It's funny how losing someone can either destroy you or make you stronger. And that bond brought Sammy, me, and Anna closer as a family. Plus, Mum makes a pretty good babysitter—which is always handy."

Janet smiles, and then stands up. "Yeah, I know how hard it raising kids. You need all the help you can get. But the government shouldn't help you. Got to do it yourself. Otherwise, what's the point of even *starting* a bloody family? All these lazy spongers, living off the country. And it's hard-working taxpayers like us who have to foot the bill. Bloody disgusting."

"Tell me about it. The idea of not working would never even cross my mind. My Dad would have *kicked my ass.*"

"Yep. You've got to set an example for your

kids. Family is everything." Janet turns to her family and smiles tenderly, and then looks back at me. "Best say your goodbyes now, Rob," she pushes the switch on the wall, and the basement is in darkness again, "because they'll be getting hungry soon."

The sound of Janet's footsteps going back up the stairs is like a dagger to the chest. "Janet. Wait. Tell me more about your family," I desperately say, clinging to the hope that I was getting through to her. "Come on, Janet! *Please!*"

But she doesn't reply. And when I hear the door closing, I'm back in a state of panic. And now even more so. With Sandra gone, and no hope of any rescue, getting through to her compassionate side really was the last throw of the dice.

I can feel my body bursting with tautness. The ropes dig in even deeper as I clench my fists tightly.

I need to get out!

Can't take it anymore!

I'm not gonna die down here!

I'll tear my own fucking arm off if I have to!

I start to tug furiously on my ropes. I can feel the flesh around them twist and burn. But the pain doesn't bother me. In fact, I can barely feel anything anymore. Not sure if it's the lack of blood circulation in my hands, or the raging adrenaline pulsating through my body.

I twist around again to face the metal pipe behind me. It's too dark to see how the rope is tied, but I pull on it nevertheless. With my feet pressed against the wall, I wrench as hard as I can. I feel the blood vessels in my neck and head about to rupture, the skin around my wrists tearing. But I don't care even if all I have left is bone! Janet Webber can have my limbs. She can take my blood.

But she's not taking Sammy!

All of a sudden I can hear the sound of something cracking. The noise spurs me on to pull even harder. And harder. I've never felt so focused, so determined, like a world champion strongman pulling a truck up a hill. Nothing's gonna stand in my way until I've split this pipe in two.

Nothing!

A sharp snapping sound propels me backwards, my head slamming onto the hard, concrete floor as I land on my back. Disorientated, I try to stand but can't; my ankles still tied firmly. But I'm free. Free of the wall. I try to pull my wrists apart, but they're still tied together. Maybe I can crawl, maybe find something sharp down here, in one of those boxes next to the washing machine. But it's too dark. I'd be feeling about almost blind. Maybe I can get to the light switch.

"Are you all right, Daddy?" Sammy asks. "What's wrong?"

"It's okay, Sammy. I'm fine. Don't worry. Just stay as quiet as you can while Daddy tries to get us out of here."

"Okay, Daddy," he whispers.

"Good boy, Sammy. I won't—" But before I can finish my sentence, something grabs my hair from behind.

It's a hand. It's ice-cold.

Another hand takes hold of the back of my collar, pulling me backwards. Choking me.

"Oh, *shit!*"

"Daddy?" Sammy calls out.

I can hear the sound of Janet's family, groaning excitedly just inches away. Using my tied wrists, I try to break the Nec's grip. But it's no use. I can feel my hair rip free from my scalp. Rolling my head frantically from side to side, I try to shake the hands off. I twist and wriggle on the floor, hoping to escape. But it's impossible. And now I can feel a third hand grab my shirt at the shoulder. The ear-piercing shrieks of animal rage fill the basement. It drowns out Sammy's cries of anguish from across the room.

In spite of my desperate attempts to free myself, I can feel my body being pulled closer to the Necs. The sound of clacking teeth is edging closer by the second, and I blindly wait for one of them to tear a chunk out of my flesh.

Not like this. Not now.

Not in the darkness.

Suddenly, the darkness vanishes and the basement has light once again. The distraction causes the Necs to loosen their grip, allowing me to pull away and roll to safety. But with Janet Webber standing at the foot of the stairs, with one hand on the light switch, and the other holding the meat cleaver, the very notion of *safety* is far from the truth.

"You fucking idiot!" Janet screams. "You had to be clever, didn't you? You had to try and get the better of me!" Before I can do anything, I see her blood-soaked foot driving towards my face. All I can do is close my eyes as it slams down into my nose. I can hear it break as the force rolls me towards Sammy. The pain is searing as I try to get to my feet. But then I feel the weight of her foot once again, this time at the side of my head. Suddenly the basement is spinning. The light in the room is fading. Lifting up my tied hands, I attempt to protect my head from another pounding. But they do nothing.

I can just about hear the voice of Sammy. He's pleading with her to stop hurting his Daddy. I see flashes of Janet's foot coming down at me. Stomp after stomp.

I feel myself slipping out of consciousness.

I fight it.

Now my eyes are closed.

Need to stay awake.

"Leave my Daddy alone!"

Suddenly my eyes are open. But the room is still

300

a blur. I blink several times, each one bringing my surroundings more and more into focus, like a Polaroid slowly forming.

The sight of the meat cleaver swinging down pulls me back into the basement. I kick out hard, managing to ram my bound feet into Janet's kneecaps. Dropping down to the floor, she screams out in agony. Before she can get back up, I scurry over to her. Reaching out, I'm able to grab her wrist, stopping her from taking another swing. She tries frantically to stand, but I manage to crawl on top of her, pinning her to the floor. I shake her wrist until the meat cleaver flies out of her grip, landing against the washing machine. Janet reaches up and wraps her fingers around my throat, choking me. Bringing my arms up, I break free from her strangulation. She tries again, so I slam my head as hard as I can down into her mouth. I hear the sound of teeth shattering as I bring my head down a second time. Janet's mouth is filled with blood. Her eyes are closing. She tries to choke me again, but her grip is too weak, so I bring both my fists down into her face, splitting her nose easily. I do it again. And again. And again.

Until her eyes are closed.

Until she stops fighting.

Until she's *fucking dead.*

I'm exhausted. I can just about catch my breath. I snap out of my frenzy. Suddenly, I'm aware of where I am—and what has just happened.

Sammy.

I turn to him. He's pressed tightly to the wall, hugging his knees into his chest, his eyes streaming with tears.

I'm sorry he had to see such violence. But it was the only way. The only way to save him. I can worry about his state of mind when we're out of this stinking basement.

And home.

I look down at Janet's still face, and then roll off her.

Meat cleaver.

I know by now, from the events of the last few days, that smashing someone's face in is never enough. So I painfully get to my feet, knees cracking, leg muscles hardly functioning, and I limp over to the washing machine. The meat-cleaver handle is poking out from under it. Just as I start to bend down to pick it up, I hear Sammy scream: "Daddy! Look out!"

Turning, I see Janet dragging her semi-conscious body towards me like a wounded Nec, clearly going for the meat cleaver. When she's just an inch from the handle, I reach up and grab the top of the generator, which is resting directly above the washing machine. I drag it off and then step back as it drops down onto Janet's head. The generator then rolls onto the hard floor, breaking the fuel cap, and spilling out a flood of petrol.

"Daddy," Sammy calls to me. "Are you all right?"

"I'm okay, boy," I reply, picking up the meat cleaver, body still pumping with adrenaline. "Let's cut those ropes off, and get you home."

I start to saw through his restraints. His wrists and ankles are rubbed raw, and bleeding, but he'll live. *Thank God.* "Now run up the stairs, Sammy. And get to the front door. But stay in the house. Whatever you do—don't go outside."

"Why, Daddy?"

"It's not safe. I'll be up in a minute, I promise. Daddy's got to do something first, okay?"

"Come with me—*I'm scared.*"

I hug him, and then kiss him on the cheek. "Don't be scared, boy. I'll be right behind you. I promise. Now off you go. As fast as you can."

His joints and muscles are clearly stiff and painful, as he gets up off the floor and hobbles over to the stairs. I clench up as he creeps past Janet's body. "Don't look at her, Sammy," I warn him. "Just go quickly. And don't go outside."

Once he's out of sight, I wedge the meat-cleaver between my thighs, and begin to vigorously rub my wrist ropes against it. After about a minute or so, I manage to free myself. Relief washes over me as I open and close my hands, trying to get a little sensation back into them. I then start to cut through my ankle ropes. The skin is a mess of blood and blister.

But I don't give a shit. I'm finally free.

It's only skin.

The petrol from the generator has now spewed all over the basement floor, right up to Sophie,

304

Malcolm, and Jack. I walk over to Janet, reach into her deep dressing-gown pocket, and pull out her cigarette lighter. Can't find the tranq gun. Must be upstairs. Or maybe she's out of ammo. I climb onto the third step of the staircase, and then push the button on the lighter. The flame pops up, and I brace to throw it onto the Necs.

This time I won't miss.

This time I'll—

"*Don't do it,*" I hear a faint, barely audible voice say, "*Please.*"

Looking down, I see Janet Webber lying on her side, staring up at me, her eyes barely open, blood running down over her face from her scalp.

"I have to, Janet."

"*Please. They're my family...I need them.*"

"I'm sorry, Janet. Your family is gone. They died a long time ago. Those things are just a disease. A disease that took them from you. You have to let them go."

"*I can't.*"

"I'm sorry, Janet. But they're dead," I throw the lighter over to the Necs, "and the dead must be

305

burnt."

The basement comes alive with blazing fire.

I watch as Janet crawls over to the burning Necs. She doesn't scream when the flames take her. Not a peep. When she reaches her family, through the inferno I see her husband biting down onto her arm. And then Sophie and Jack claw at her sweltering flesh.

The heat becomes too much to endure, so I run up the stairs to the door. Once through the doorway, I quickly close it.

It's daytime. Feels like morning. Have no way of knowing, though. So disorientating.

"Sammy!" I call out as I make my way along the hallway. "You okay, boy?"

"I'm okay, Daddy," he tells me, just as I see him standing next to the front door, just like I told him to. "Good boy," I say, as I get to him and hug him—*tighter than I've ever hugged him before.* I can't believe we made it. It's overwhelming.

But it's not over yet.

Got to get the fuck out of this house!

Maybe we don't have to. Maybe we could just

ride it out until the cavalry shows up. But how long is *that* gonna take? Don't fancy spending the night here with that fire burning. And what if the cavalry *doesn't* show up? What then?

Have to find the tranq gun.

It's got to be around here somewhere. Maybe it's upstairs by the front window. Or in the kitchen. Need to search the—

The entire house shakes with the rumble of an explosion.

The basement! Must have burnt through a gas pipe!

Oh, shit!

I look down the hallway and see that the basement door has been blown completely off its hinges. Smoke and flames climb out of the doorway. *Need to leave now!*

"I'm scared, Daddy," Sammy says, clasping at my legs. "The house is on fire!"

"Don't worry, boy. Daddy's here."

Fuck, I wish I had that *bloody* tranq gun.

Within seconds, the hallway is filled with smoke and flames. I quickly guard him against the scorching heat.

"We're gonna have to make a run for it, Sammy," I tell him, as calmly as possible. "I can carry you, but if you see some people outside, just close your eyes. I promise they won't hurt you. Okay?"

Sammy nods, tears streaming down his face.

The fire is now inches away from us, spitting angrily at the back of my neck.

Picking him up off the floor, I wince from the searing pain in my wrists. I unlock the front door and then place my hand on the handle.

"Ready?" I say. "One…two…*three!*"

I leap out onto the pavement and then run onto the road. The cold winter breeze hits me straight away. But it feels good to be outside. To breathe fresh air. Away from the blaze.

Away from that *fucking* basement.

Just halfway across the road, I stop in my tracks. My heart sinks with horror at the sight.

An army of Necs is clustered about twenty metres up from us.

Thank God Sammy's head is over my shoulder,

facing in the opposite direction. Can't let him see this. Not after everything. It's too much.

I've never seen so many gathered together, as if ready to charge at us like a stampede of bulls, pulsating with rage.

Must be a *hundred* of them.

How is this even possible?

The explosion?

Not sure whether I should make a run for it. Break into one of these houses. Any house. Or stay completely still.

Can't think straight.

I'm frozen.

Can't make a decision.

Have to...

"Look, Daddy!" Sammy cries into my ear. "Look behind you!"

I turn to look down Marbleview Street, expecting to see another horde of Necs. But instead, I see something that makes me gasp with emotion.

Thirty, maybe even fifty riot police are stood, all lined up in rows, armed with large, transparent shields—and guns.

Lots of guns.

The cavalry!

I race over to a parked car and duck down as the police charge at the Necs. The deafening sound of guns firing, and bodies crashing into riot shields causes me to pull Sammy in close and cover his ears from the noise.

But the noise doesn't bother me. Instead, it fills me with hope—and an overwhelming sense of relief.

Never before have I been so happy to see so many police; to listen to the roar of helicopters above me; to hear the growls of a riot, just metres from my front door.

Any other day, I might have picked up a shield and joined the fight, to drive the dead from my home.

But not this time.

I gently stroke Sammy's hair as I wait for the battle to be over. Wait for a chance to slip away to somewhere safer.

Anywhere but Marbleview street.

It's time to get the hell out of here.

Fuck you, Crandale!

And *fuck you*, Janet Webber!

EPILOGUE

"Inspection's coming up again," Stuart informs me. "Need to be on our best behaviour. Can't let our standards slip now. The company's been talking about merging us with Birmingham. And you know what that means—more job losses."

"No worries, Stuart," I tell him, only half-listening. "Will do."

Stuart does a quick inventory count, pointing his pen at each stretcher. "Only twenty-six today, Robert. Not too bad then." He smiles tightly, and then leaves the room.

"Yeah, wonderful," I say, as I watch him disappear outside.

"*Prick*," I whisper, when I'm positive he's out of range.

I take a look at the stretchers, and then at the time on the wall. Twenty-six. Not the end of the world. I'll be out by seven. *Hopefully*.

I grab a pair of safety-goggles from the shelf and slip them over my eyes, and then cover my mouth and nose with a plastic mask. I walk up to the control panel, turn the dial to green, and then flip the main switch. There's a loud rumble as the furnace ignites. Instantly, I can feel the heat radiate from the sides of the heavy furnace door. The noise circulates the room, causing the metal stretchers to roll and rattle into each other.

The first body bag is moving already. *Bloody tranqs.* Useless. Need to be stronger.

Cheap imports.

I stop myself reaching for the zip. Have to fight the urge. I start to wheel the body over to the furnace door. Opening the heavy door, a gust of eyebrow-singeing heat hits me in the face. Despite the goggles, I close my eyes and wipe the beads of sweat from my forehead. I roll the yellow body bag off the stretcher and onto the platform, and then push the platform inside. I slam the door shut and lock it. The furnace comes alive when I press the large red button, incinerating the bag in seconds.

One down. Twenty-five more to go.

Another day. Another dollar.

It's a dirty job.

But someone's got to do it.

COMING SOON
FROM STEVEN JENKINS

BURN THE DEAD: PURGE

BURN THE DEAD: RIOT

To receive emails on all future book releases, please subscribe to: www.steven-jenkins.com

About the Author

Steven Jenkins was born in the small Welsh town of Llanelli, where he began writing stories at the age of eight, inspired by '80s horror movies and novels by *Richard Matheson*.

During Steven's teenage years, he became a great lover of writing dark and twisted poems—six of which gained him publications with *Poetry Now*, *Brownstone Books*, and *Strong Words*.

Over the next few years, as well as becoming a husband and father, Steven spent his free time writing short stories, achieving further publication with *Dark Moon Digest*. His terrifying tales of the afterlife and zombies gained him positive reviews, particularly his story, *Burning Ambition*, which also came runner up in a *Five-Stop-Story* contest. And in 2014 his debut novel, *Fourteen Days* was published by Barking Rain Press.

You can find out more about Steven Jenkins at his website: www.steven-jenkins.com or on Facebook: www.facebook.com/stevenjenkinsauthor and on Twitter: twitter.com/Author_Jenkins

OTHER TITLES
BY STEVEN JENKINS

FOURTEEN DAYS

Workaholic developer Richard Gardener is laid up at home for two week's mandatory leave—doctor's orders. No stress. No computers. Just fourteen days of complete rest.

Bliss for most, but hell for Richard... in more ways than one. There's a darkness that lives inside Richard's home; a presence he never knew existed because he was seldom there alone.

Did he just imagine those footsteps? The smoke alarm shrieking?

The woman in his kitchen?

His wife thinks that he's just suffering from work withdrawal, but as the days crawl by in his solitary confinement, the terror seeping through the walls continues to escalate—threatening his health, his sanity, and his marriage.

When the inconceivable no longer seems quite so impossible, Richard struggles to come to terms with what is happening and find a way to banish the darkness—before he becomes an exile in his own home.

"Gripping, tense, and bloody scary. The author has taken the classic ghost story, and blended it faultlessly with Hitchcock's Rear Window."

COLIN DAVIES
DIRECTOR OF BBC'S BAFTA
WINNING: THE COALHOUSE

"Fourteen Days is the most purely enjoyable novel I've read in a very long time."

RICHARD BLANDFORD
THE WRITER'S WORKSHOP &
AUTHOR OF HOUND DOG

Available at:

www.steven-jenkins.com,

Amazon UK, Amazon US,

and all other book retailers.

SPINE

Listen closely. A creak, almost too light to be heard...was it the shifting of an old house, or footsteps down the hallway? Breathe softly, and strain to hear through the silence. That breeze against your neck might be a draught, or an open window.

Slip into the pages of SPINE and you'll be persuaded to leave the lights on and door firmly bolted. From Steven Jenkins, bestselling author of *Fourteen Days* and *Burn the Dead*, this horror collection of eight stories go beyond the realm of terror to an entirely different kind of creepiness. Beneath innocent appearances lurk twisted minds and scary monsters, from soft scratches behind the wall, to the paranoia of walking through a crowd and knowing that every single eye is locked on you. In this world, voices lure lost souls to the cliff's edge and illicit drugs offer glimpses of things few should see. Scientists tamper with the afterlife, and the strange happenings at a nursing home are not what they first seem.

So don't let that groan from the closet fool you—the monster is hiding right where you least expect it.

"If you love scary campfire stories of ghosts, demonology, and all things that go bump in the night, then you'll love this horror collection by author Steven Jenkins."

COLIN DAVIES
DIRECTOR OF BBC'S BAFTA
WINNING: THE COALHOUSE

Available at:

www.steven-jenkins.com,

Amazon UK, Amazon US,

and all other book retailers.

ROTTEN BODIES

We all fear death's dark spectre, but in a zombie apocalypse, dying is a privilege reserved for the lucky few. There are worse things than a bullet to the brain—*much* worse.

The dead are walking, and they're hungry. Steven Jenkins, bestselling author of *Fourteen Days* and *Burn The Dead*, shares six zombie tales that are rotten for all the right reasons.

Meet Dave, a husband and father with a dirty secret, who quickly discovers that lies aren't only dangerous…they're deadly. Athlete Sarah once ran for glory, but when she finds herself alone on a country road with an injured knee, second place is as good as last. Working in a cremation facility, Rob likes to peek secretly at the faces of his inventory before they're turned to ash. When it comes to workplace health and sanity, however, some rules are better left unbroken. Howard, shovelling coal in the darkness of a Welsh coal mine, knows something's amiss when his colleagues begin to disappear. But it's when the lights come on that things get truly scary.

Six different takes on the undead, from the grotesque to the downright terrifying. But reader beware: as the groans get louder and the twitching starts, you'll be *dying* to reach the final page.

"Utterly hair-raising, in all its gory glory!"

CATE HOGAN

AUTHOR OF ONE SUMMER

Available at:

and all other book retailers.